- You can return this item to any Bournemouth library but not all libraries are open every day.

- Items must be returned on or before the due date. Please note that you will be charged for items returned late.

- Items may be renewed unless requested by another customer.

- Renewals can be made in any library, by telephone, email or online via the website. Your membership card number and PIN will be required.

- Please look after this item - you may be charged for any damage.

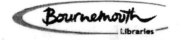

Bournemouth Libraries

www.bournemouth.gov.uk/libraries

She should look away. Step back. Close the door. Lock it.

Instead she stood there, a doe trapped in headlights. "Christo." His name on her lips was barely more than a whisper. She paused and ran her tongue over them. The very air seemed to shimmer between them.

"Send me away." His voice was harsh.

She frowned at the tone. "What?"

His jaw tightened. "You heard me, Nat. Tell me to go."

She hesitated, then drew a breath, steadying herself. She knew what he was demanding. And she knew the wisdom of it. But she couldn't do it.

Award-winning author **Anne McAllister** was once given a blueprint for happiness that included a nice, literate husband, a ramshackle Victorian house, a horde of mischievous children, a bunch of big, friendly dogs, and a life spent writing stories about tall, dark and handsome heroes. 'Where do I sign up?' she asked, and promptly did. Lots of years later, she's happy to report the blueprint was a success. She's always happy to share the latest news with readers at her website, www.annemcallister.com, and welcomes their letters there, or at PO Box 3904, Bozeman, Montana 59772, USA (SASE appreciated).

ONE-NIGHT MISTRESS... CONVENIENT WIFE

BY
ANNE McALLISTER

First published in Great Britain 2009
Harlequin Mills & Boon Limited,
Eton House, 18-24 Paradise Road, Richmond, Surrey TW9 1SR

© Barbara Schenck 2009

ISBN: 978 0 263 20843 6

Set in Times Roman 10½ on 12¾ pt
07-0909-48756

Harlequin Mills & Boon policy is to use papers that are natural, renewable and recyclable products and made from wood grown in sustainable forests. The logging and manufacturing process conform to the legal environmental regulations of the country of origin.

Printed and bound in Great Britain
by CPI Antony Rowe, Chippenham, Wiltshire

ONE-NIGHT MISTRESS... CONVENIENT WIFE

CHAPTER ONE

NATALIE pulled her car into the garage below her mother's apartment, shut off the engine—and felt a panic unlike anything she'd felt in the last three years.

"Wholly unnecessary," she told herself firmly out loud because the truth of the assertion stood a better chance of making it past her nerves if she heard the spoken words. If she heard them, she thought, she might even believe them.

Actually, in her mind she did believe them.

But what she believed logically and what her guts were telling her was not even close to the same thing.

"Don't be stupid," she said. "It is absolutely no big deal."

And it wasn't. She was cat-sitting, for goodness' sake! She was watering a few plants and living in her mother's apartment for two or three weeks because her mother had to go to Iowa to take care of her own mother after a hip-replacement operation. And while the cat was portable, the seven-foot rubber-tree plant was not.

"Harry was supposed to do it," Laura Ross had explained apologetically on the phone very early this morning. "You know, the boy across the way? But he broke his leg skate-boarding last night. Spiral fracture, his mother said. Not even a walking cast yet. I'm sorry to have to ask you—"

"No. It's all right," Natalie had made herself say. "Of course I'll do it. I'll be glad to," she'd lied.

So here she was.

All she had to do was get out of the car, go around the building, up the steps to her mother's apartment, open the door and go in.

She'd done it once already today. She'd come to pick her mother up to take her to the airport late this morning and it had been perfectly straightforward. No worries at all.

Because there had been no danger of running into Christo Savas then.

Chances were, Natalie assured herself, she wouldn't run into him now, either.

What was the possibility, after all, that she would be rounding the building to go up the stairs at the very moment her mother's landlord—and boss—was coming up the walk to his house or stepping out on his back porch?

Slim, she decided. None was preferable, of course. Please God she would not see him at all these next two or three weeks.

But even if she did, she reminded herself, she was an adult. She could smile at him politely and go her own way. And it didn't matter what he would be thinking. It didn't matter at all!

"Right," she said now in the no-nonsense tone her mother had used all the time Natalie was growing up. "Grass never gets cut by looking at the mower," she would say when Natalie or her brother Dan balked at doing the chore. It had since become a family slogan applied to any reluctance to get the job done. Laura would be saying it now.

Of course her mother had no idea why Natalie had

spent the last three years avoiding Christo Savas—and she never would.

Taking one last deep breath, Natalie got out of the car, being careful not to let the door bump against Christo's Jaguar next to it. It was the same one he'd had three years ago.

Once she'd ridden in that car with the top down, had tipped her head back and felt the wind in her hair, had laughed and slanted a glance at the man driving and had dared to dream ridiculous dreams.

Now she turned away and shut her own car door with a bit more firmness than absolutely necessary. Then she opened the back, grabbed her laptop case and the suitcase with the clothes she'd brought, shut it and, heart still pounding more rapidly than she wished, she opened the door to the small walled garden.

It was empty.

She breathed again. Then, with barely a glance toward Christo's big house on the far side of what her mother had turned into the closest thing southern California probably had to an 'olde English garden,' she made a sharp right and quickly climbed the wooden stairs that led to Laura's apartment over the garage.

Once on the porch, she had a view down the broad street that led to The Strand and the beach beyond. It was empty. She set down her suitcase and laptop and fumbled in her purse for her mother's key.

It was nearly six. Her mother had said Christo usually went surfing right after work—"to decompress," Laura had told her—and then came back for dinner which they ate at six-thirty.

"You eat with him?" Natalie had said when her mother

imparted this surprising information. Her brows had lifted in dismay—and consternation.

Laura had gone right on packing her bags. "I don't like cooking for one."

"You cook for him?"

"I cook for myself," her mother said primly in the face of Natalie's undisguised disapproval. "And I make enough for two."

"Well, I'm not cooking for him," Natalie said firmly.

"Of course not." Her mother dismissed the notion. "He wouldn't expect it."

No, Natalie thought, *and he wouldn't want it, either.*

"He doesn't even know you're going to be here," her mother had gone on, brightening Natalie's day considerably. "He knew I had arranged for Harry to come. But when Carol, Harry's mother called this morning, I didn't even tell Christo because I knew he'd feel responsible. He'd think he needed to take care of Herbie and do the plants, and he couldn't possibly. He's much too busy for that."

Well, perhaps the day wasn't all that bright. But Natalie knew her mother was telling the truth. She didn't have to be reminded how hard Christo Savas worked. She'd seen it firsthand. And if he didn't know she was here, even better. Perhaps she could keep it that way.

Her fingers found the ring of keys. She picked out her mother's, stuck it in the keyhole, gave it a twist, and pushed open the door. Then with one last quick glance down toward the ocean where, yes indeed, she could see silhouetted against the bright sun a muscular man with a surfboard just coming up the beach, she picked up her laptop and her suitcase, hurried inside and banged the door.

In the blessed shadowed coolness of the small entryway

she dropped her bags, shut her eyes and took a deep relieved breath.

"Natalie?" The voice was gruff, masculine and sounded as shocked and disbelieving as her own ears were.

Her eyes snapped open. She blinked rapidly, trying to accustom them to the dim indoor light, to see the cool empty living room she expected, to see Herbie the cat, whom she expected.

Not to see the man who had been crouched by the fireplace and was now straightening, drawing himself up to his full six feet two inches and staring at her with narrowed suspicious eyes.

Her mouth felt as if someone had suddenly dumped a pail full of sand in it. "Christo?" She barely choked his name out. Then she frowned, too.

Their gazes met, locked. And then, in unison, "What the hell are you doing here?" they said.

"I live here. There," he corrected, jerking his head toward the house beyond the garden. His gaze went to the suitcase by her feet. "What's that for?"

The suspicion in his voice rankled. Natalie stood straighter. "I'm moving in," she said, pleased at how firm her voice sounded. "Temporarily."

Christo's brows drew down. "What for?"

"I'm taking care of Herbie. And the plants."

"Your mother said Harry—"

"Harry broke his leg."

Now the brows went up. "First I've heard about it." There was clear disbelief in his voice. He rested an arm against the mantel of the fireplace and regarded her doubtfully.

Natalie drew herself together. "Feel free to go over to

Harry's and ask. You might be right. Maybe this is all some great plot of my mother's to throw me and you together."

Christo grunted at the scorn in her tone. "She wouldn't do that."

"No, she wouldn't." Laura might well be thinking that it was a good idea for her twenty-five-year-old daughter to start looking around for a husband, but she wouldn't meddle. Natalie was sure of that.

"I can feed the cat and water the plants." Christo's tone made it sound not like a suggestion. It sounded like an order.

Natalie bristled. She'd already survived the part she wanted to avoid. "I'm sure you can," she said starchily. "But my mother didn't ask you. She asked me. And I'm doing it."

His teeth came together. She imagined she could hear them grinding. Well, so be it.

"So we know what I'm doing here," she said pointedly. "What about you? You don't just habitually wander into my mother's apartment, I hope."

The teeth did grind, then. "No, I don't habitually wander into her apartment. I was measuring for bookshelves." He held out his hand. There was a measuring tape in it.

"Bookshelves?" Natalie echoed doubtfully.

"She's always saying to me how much she loves this room, but that it would be perfect if it had bookcases on either side of the fireplace." He shrugged, but also jerked his head toward the space behind him and, studying the space, Natalie could see her mother's point. His mouth twisted. "A belated birthday surprise."

Natalie was surprised he knew her mother's birthday had been last week. "And you were going to have them put in while she was gone?"

"No. I was going to put them in myself while she was gone."

They stared at each other. An awareness Natalie didn't want to acknowledge arced between them. It had been there ever since she'd heard his voice and opened her eyes to see him standing there. It was a feeling she'd felt with no one else—ever. Once she'd thought she understood it. Had cultivated it. Relished it.

Now she wanted nothing whatever to do with it at all.

"Well, you can't," she said and folded her arms across her chest.

His jaw worked, but he didn't say anything. Their gazes were still locked and Natalie refused to be the one to look away first. Not this time. She was in the right this time.

"Fine," he said shortly. "I'll finish measuring now. I'll order the wood. I'll put them up when she gets back, mess up the living room while she's here." He turned and knelt back down, ignoring her. In effect, dismissing her.

Natalie glared at his back. Why had she ever thought she wanted to spend the rest of her life with this man? Why had she ever been in love with him?

She hadn't, she told herself sharply. She'd been infatuated, the victim of a law-school clerk's foolish crush on a brilliant up-and-coming litigator. She'd been dazzled by his brilliance, his extraordinary good looks, and whatever perverse sexual chemistry had always seemed to hum between them whenever he was in the room.

And the kiss, her mental memory box reminded her. *Don't forget the kiss!*

No, God help her, she couldn't forget the kiss. Try as she would she'd never been able to forget entirely the moment she and Christo Savas had locked lips. It had been the most blazingly hot kiss of her then twenty-two years. The most blazingly hot *anything* of her entire life—even up to this very moment.

It had been the impulse that had spurred on her unutterably foolish action that night three years ago.

Action she was not about to repeat no matter what Christo Savas thought. And it was no secret, Natalie knew, staring at him now, what he thought.

"All right," she said abruptly. "Go ahead and put in the bookshelves."

He was kneeling on the floor, about to measure. But he slanted her a quick glance, and in it she saw the instant wariness she expected.

She gave him a saccharine smile. "Don't worry. I'll stay completely out of your way. Won't bother you at all. Won't invite you to my bed and won't turn up in yours. You're perfectly safe." She made her tone sound mocking.

But they both knew she wasn't mocking him. She was mocking herself, the hopelessly naive girl who had taken a summer's working relationship, a sense of kindredness that was, in retrospect, obviously one-sided, and a single spontaneous kiss to celebrate a triumph in the courtroom as an indication of something far deeper. A girl who had thought he must love her the way she imagined she loved him—and who had actually gone to his bed to prove it.

She made herself smile and hold his unblinking jade-green gaze, willing him to believe it because, God knew, it was the truth. There was no way on earth she would ever make a fool of herself like that again!

"If you're sure…" Christo began.

"Of course I'm sure." She gathered her laptop case and the suitcase up into her arms, fleetingly aware that she was probably using them as armor, even as she carried them into the room. "I was just…surprised to see you. In here," she qualified because she didn't want him thinking she'd been intending to avoid him—even if she had been.

She set the laptop case on her mother's dining-room table. "I'll just put this away." She nodded down at the suitcase, then turned toward the bedroom. "And I'll come back and help you measure."

"I don't need any help," he said in a tone that brooked no argument.

Which meant that, even though she'd pretty much spelled it out, he still didn't entirely trust her not to fling herself at him even now.

"Fine. Suit yourself." Natalie shrugged and carried the suitcase into the bedroom, only sagging down onto the bed and letting out a shuddering breath once she got there.

She could, of course, just leave the suitcase on the bed and deal with the contents later. But rushing back into a room where she clearly wasn't wanted—and didn't want to be—was not the best idea.

And there was a whole lot to recommend staying right where she was. She could use the time to put her clothes away—and regain her equilibrium in the process.

She hadn't wanted to run into Christo at all. She'd done her best to avoid him for the past three years because she still writhed in mortification every time she thought about that night in his apartment.

That night she'd waited for him in his bed.

Even now her cheeks burned at the memory.

That he'd been shocked to find her there when he got home from a business dinner that night went without saying. She'd expected that.

But she'd also expected he'd be pleased. Delighted, in fact. And happy to join her.

Wrong. A hundred thousand times wrong. And if the circumstances had been mortifying, it was how badly she'd misread the situation that she still had trouble facing. She wasn't used to being a fool.

Well, he needn't worry, she thought as she got up and began taking her clothes out of the suitcase, hanging them in the closet, trying not to hear every sound he made as he moved in the living room.

She certainly wouldn't be jumping into his bed again.

But it would be a whole lot easier if her earlier humiliation and subsequent hard-won maturity were complemented now by total indifference to the man in the other room.

Sadly, they weren't.

Something about Christo Savas still had the ability to make her heart quicken in her chest. His thick dark hair perhaps? His chiseled jaw and sculpted cheekbones? His sharp straight nose and fathomless green eyes? His rangy but muscular body that looked as appealing today in faded jeans and a gray T-shirt as it had in tropical-weight wool suits, starched long-sleeved shirts and ties?

All of the above?

Unfortunately, yes.

But it was even more than that. Always had been.

If Christo's arresting good looks had first attracted Natalie's attention the summer she'd been a clerk in the firm where her father was a partner, it had very quickly become more than his hard body and handsome face that held her interest.

His quiet intensity, determined hard work and steel-trap mind were equally appealing. So were his incisive arguments and his way with words. She'd been dazzled by the young litigator and it hadn't taken long to become smitten.

She'd been raised on the story of her own parents' courtship and marriage—*He was a young lawyer and I was working in the office. It was love at first sight,* Laura used to tell her children. So Natalie hadn't found it hard to believe in a variation on the same theme for herself and Christo.

Bolstered by her own family history, and aware of a certain electricity in the air every time she and Christo Savas looked at one another, Natalie had seen their relationship as fate.

And she'd done her best to make history repeat itself.

It hadn't been easy. Christo had been consumed with work, not with the summer clerk in the securities department. They had rarely been in the same room as each other, though she did help out with extensive legal research in a securities case he was trying.

She might never have fallen into the trap of her own illusion if she hadn't found him in the law library late one afternoon flipping through books, and scowling as he made furious notes and muttered under his breath.

"Something wrong?" she'd ventured.

"Not something," he'd said grimly. "Everything."

He'd just been appointed guardian *ad litem* for a seven-year-old boy named Jonas in the middle of a nasty billion-dollar divorce and custody case. "I don't know anything about family law! I don't know anything about kids! I don't even know where to start."

That wasn't true, of course. He knew plenty, and certainly enough to figure out where to start. He was just frustrated, overwhelmed. Momentarily vulnerable.

And Natalie, heart beating like a hummingbird's wings,

had offered, "I could do some research if you'd like. On my own time. It would be good practice," she added, smiling hopefully at him. And then she'd felt it again, that current of electricity arcing between them, when he met her gaze and nodded slowly.

"Yeah," he'd said. "If you wouldn't mind. I'll tell you what I need."

For the next three weeks, she had worked her tail off for him. Lunch hours, evenings, weekends. She'd spent every waking moment that she wasn't being a clerk with her nose in a book or scowling at a computer screen scribbling furiously, then reporting her findings to Christo who was almost always in his office just as late.

"You're a star," he'd told her when she found some particularly helpful cases. And he'd been almost as grateful for the pastrami sandwiches she brought in because he never took time to eat.

He'd been willing to stop and explain things to her when she dared to ask questions. And sometimes when she found something and let out a little yelp of joy, he'd come over and bend over her shoulder so close that she could feel his breath stir the tendrils of her hair.

"Great. I can use this." And she'd looked up to see a grin on his face and a determined light in his eye. Once more their gazes had caught and held.

And Natalie had dared to believe.

But she wouldn't have believed without the kiss.

It came without warning the day he'd got Jonas's formerly intractable parents to finally see the light and realize it was a child they were dealing with, not a silver service or an Oriental rug. She'd been in the parking garage, heading for her car late that afternoon when he'd got out of his, coming from a meeting about Jonas. She'd paused, waiting for him to get out, expecting yet more bad news. But the look of sheer joy on his face when he shut the door and came toward her was one she'd never forget.

Her heart kicked over. "Did they—?" she began.

The grin nearly split his face. "They did. At last." And suddenly he was there in front of her, and what had begun as a grin and a high-five turned into a fierce exultant hug.

Instinctively she had lifted her face to smile into his— and they had kissed.

Natalie might have been only twenty-two and not the world's most experienced woman, but she knew there were kisses and there were kisses.

This kiss might have started out as pure exultation, the shared joy of something going right. But in a second it was something very different indeed. Just as a single simple spark could become a conflagration, so it was the moment their lips touched.

She'd never felt it before.

The kiss didn't last. Barely a second or two later he let her go and stepped back abruptly, looking around as if expecting to be shot. If anyone had seen them, she knew he could have been—not shot—but facing the wrath of the senior partners and the possible loss of his job.

"You'd better go on home," he said hoarsely, and without a backward glance he strode off across the garage toward the elevator.

Natalie didn't move. She'd simply stood there, her fingers pressed against her lips, holding on to the memory, the sensation, the dawning belief that there was substance to the dreams of the future she'd hoped for.

Of course, it had been only a matter of moments. But

with one single kiss Christo Savas had nearly burned her to the ground. Even now, running her tongue over her lips, she could still taste—

"Er-mm."

At the throat-clearing sound behind her, Natalie whipped around, face burning. Christo stood in the doorway to her mother's bedroom watching her.

"What?" she snapped.

"I'm finished measuring. I'll order the wood in the morning. Then I have to sand and stain it before I can put it in. I'll give you plenty of warning." He sounded very businesslike, very proper.

Exactly the way she wanted him. She gave a short curt nod. "Thank you." Then, because she knew it was true, and she also knew that, despite her own feelings about Christo Savas, he had done her mother numerous good turns over the past three years, she added, "My mother will appreciate it."

"I hope so. I like your mother."

"Yes." The feeling was mutual. Laura thought the sun rose and set on Christo Savas. She couldn't understand why Natalie declined invitations that included him.

Still they stared at each other. And there it was again, that damned electricity, that unfortunate awareness. And still he didn't leave.

Maybe they needed to clarify things further. "My mother said you'd water the plants in the garden."

He nodded. "She thought it might be too much for Harry."

"I'm sure she was right. But since Harry's out of the picture, I can do them. I'm not currying favor—" she said awkwardly.

"Let's leave it the way she arranged it."

All lines neatly drawn. Everyone in their own place. "All right."

At last he turned toward the living room, then glanced back at her over his shoulder. "Maybe I'll see you around."

"Maybe." Natalie didn't move. Watched his back disappear, heard his footsteps recede, the door open and close, the sound of his feet on the steps outside. Only then did she breathe again, and say aloud what she was really thinking. "Not if I see you first."

Natalie Ross.

As gorgeous and enticing as ever. Right on his bloody damn doorstep.

Christo tipped back in his desk chair, let out a sigh, rubbed the heels of his hands against his eyes, then leaned forward and tried to focus again.

It didn't work. He'd been trying to focus all evening. Ordinarily that wasn't a problem. He regularly settled down and worked well after dinner when it was quiet and there were no clients in and out, no phone calls, no papers to sign or distractions lurking and he could concentrate.

Not tonight.

Tonight every time he tried to bend his mind around where Teresa Holton's soon-to-be-ex-husband might have secreted assets everyone knew he had, his mind—no, worse, his hormones—had other ideas.

They wanted to focus on Natalie.

It was because he'd been too absorbed with work lately, he told himself. Except for an hour or so of surfing most evenings after work, he hadn't taken any time off in weeks. His hormones were feeling deprived as well. It had been two months since Ella, the woman who, for the past year or so, had regularly been the object of their attention, decided she wanted more than a casual no-strings affair.

As Christo didn't—a fact that he had made crystal-clear from the beginning—he had let her go without a qualm. But he'd had neither the time nor the inclination to look for anyone else since.

He didn't have the time now.

As for inclination, if his hormones were inclined toward Natalie Ross, too damn bad. There was no woman on earth less likely to want a no-strings affair than Natalie. She was her mother's daughter through and through.

Though Laura and Clayton Ross were now divorced, it had never been Laura's idea. It was Clayton who'd run off with the paralegal, leaving Laura, after twenty-five years of marriage, to fend for herself. She had, but she still believed in marriage and babies and forever. So did Natalie. Christo knew it instinctively.

He wanted nothing of the sort.

Resolutely he picked up his pencil again and beat a tattoo on the desktop, trying to stimulate brain cells. But his brain cells didn't need stimulation. They had plenty, thank you very much. It just wasn't focused on the Holton case. They had something—*someone*—else in mind.

As did another part of his anatomy.

Irritated, Christo shoved away from the desk and stood up, flexing his shoulders and pacing around the room.

His office was at the back of the house with a wide window facing Laura's garden. It was dark now. He couldn't see the flowers. But if he looked up, he could see the light on in Laura's apartment. The drapes were pulled, but Natalie could, if she were so inclined, look between them directly down into his office. She could watch him pace.

Christo walked across the room and flipped the blinds shut. He wished he could as easily shut out thoughts of her.

He knew, of course, that Laura hadn't been trying to complicate his life by asking her daughter to come and take care of the cat and the plants. Laura was as protective of his time as he was himself. More so, in this case, because if she hadn't been she'd have asked him to take care of the cat and the plants when Harry broke his leg.

Instead she'd asked her daughter.

Of course, she had no idea about his history with Natalie.

Not that there was a history. There had very determinedly—on his part—*not* been any history at all.

Except for that one disastrous totally spontaneous kiss.

He scrubbed his hands over his face now, remembering it.

He had never done anything so stupid before or since. He'd always been absolutely impeccable in his workplace behavior. And if the parking garage had not been precisely part of the workplace, that was pretty much legal hairsplitting and Christo knew it. Natalie had been working at the firm, and if he wasn't her boss he was certainly senior on the totem pole—and he damned well should have known better.

He had known better.

It had simply been a combination of joy and relief. And desire.

Time to call a spade a spade. But doing so didn't make the desire go away. Old memories welled up. He squashed them. Memories of scant hours ago took their place. He resisted them, too.

He prowled some more. He cracked his knuckles, then pressed his palms down against the desktop, hunching his shoulders and staring blankly down at the paper he'd given up trying to make notes on. He couldn't even see what he'd written so far. Visions of Natalie teased at the corners of his mind.

"Stop it," he told himself sharply.

It was perverse, this desire he felt for Natalie Ross's slender yet curvy body—as perverse now as it had been the first time.

Christo didn't do rampant desire. He liked women—in their place. Which was not in his mind or in a relationship. Only in his bed.

He hadn't lusted madly after any female since his teens. Now, at the age of thirty-two, he should be well over that sort of thing. He *was* well over it!

He'd walked away from Natalie Ross once, for God's sake. He'd done the right thing. The sensible thing. The *only* thing.

Now he gave up trying to work. He went out the front door and crossed The Strand, dropping down onto the path along the beach and beginning to run.

So, fine. The words pounded in his head as he picked up the pace. He'd resisted Natalie Ross before. He'd simply do it again.

CHAPTER TWO

For three days Natalie didn't see Christo at all.

Well, that wasn't quite true. She caught a glimpse or two of him in the morning as he headed off to work while she was taking her time, deliberately not venturing out of the apartment, staying in to feed the cat and do some scheduling work on her laptop for the rent-a-wife business she ran with her cousin, while she incidentally kept one eye on the window so she could see when he had left.

In the evening of the second day she saw him down on the patio of the garden sanding the boards that had been delivered for her mother's bookcases.

That had been more than a glimpse. In fact, she'd stood there, unable to tear her eyes away from the sight of a shirtless Christo Savas bending over a board, a sheen of sweat glinting across his bare muscular back as he sanded the wood vigorously, then straightened and smoothed his hand along the grain.

She'd lingered in the window until his cell phone rang and in answering it, he turned and his gaze lifted to meet hers.

Instantly, Natalie stepped back, face burning at being caught out ogling him. She nearly tripped over Herbie in her haste to retreat to the kitchen where she poured herself a tall glass of ice water which she drank right down.

She stayed well away from the window after that, not venturing near until the sun had set and the world was completely dark.

The next day she didn't see him at all. She got back to the apartment shortly before suppertime, expecting that she might run into him in the patio and steeling herself for the encounter. But he was nowhere to be seen, and the boards were stacked in the garage, still awaiting stain.

The next evening she didn't see him, either.

Her mother rang that night. "I would have called sooner," she said, "but I didn't want you to think I was hovering."

Natalie smiled. "Thank you for the vote of confidence."

"So how are things going? Does Herbie miss me?"

"Of course. But things are fine. Herbie is thriving. The plants are surviving."

"Of course they are," her mother said with quiet satis-faction. "I knew I could count on you. How's Christo?"

"What?" The unexpectedness of the question made Natalie's voice crack.

"I wondered how Christo was coping," Laura said. "I know you aren't feeding him dinner, but I thought you might have talked to him, found out how things are going."

"He doesn't appear to be starving," Natalie said drily. "So I assume he's getting nourishment." But then, because she knew her mother would wonder at her edgy tone, she said, "I really haven't seen him to talk to, Mom. Only once, the day I got here."

"Well, I hope things are going all right at work," her mother said. "The temp who usually helps out is working elsewhere. So I had to train another woman before I left.

It should be fine," she said, but her voice trailed off and she sounded a little worried.

Natalie steeled herself against it. "You'll have to ask Christo about that," she said briskly.

"I have," Laura said. "I called him tonight. He said everything was under control."

"Then you should believe him."

"I know. I do." A pause. "But he sounded—I don't know—stressed. I hope he'd let me know if it wasn't all right," Laura added pensively. "Oh, drat. There's the bell again."

"Bell?"

Her mother let out a weary sigh. "Your grandmother has a bell. She rings it when she wants something."

"Let me guess. She wants things often." Natalie smiled at the thought of her imperious grandmother ringing a bell to make her mother jump. It would delight the old lady no end.

"Every other minute," Laura concurred. "Coming, Mother. I'll give you a call in a few days," she said to Natalie. "Wish me luck."

Natalie hung up and was silently wishing her mother luck when there was a knock on her front door.

She opened it to find Christo standing there, still in the dark trousers and long-sleeved dress shirt he would have worn to work. The top button was undone, his tie was askew, and he had his suit coat slung over his shoulder.

"Your mother says you run a rent-a-wife agency," he said without preamble.

Natalie blinked in surprise. But she stopped herself before she wetted dry lips. "That's right," she said.

"Do you rent office personnel, too?"

"Office…"

"I need someone to take your mother's place." His jaw worked.

"I thought everything was under control?"

When he narrowed his gaze at her, Natalie shrugged. "I just got off the phone with my mother. She said she'd talked to you and that you said everything was fine."

"I lied." He dropped his jacket over the porch railing and raked fingers through already mussed hair. "They didn't work out."

"They?"

"The first one was bossy to the kids. Acted like she was some damn mother superior."

Kids? It took Natalie a moment to realize what he was talking about. When she thought about Christo she generally still thought of him at her father's firm, but of course he wasn't there. He'd left not long after she had at the end of that summer to go off on his own—to start his own practice in which he focused on family law. Because of Jonas? She'd often wondered. But of course she'd never found that out.

Now he said, "I sent her back, and they sent me another one. One your mother hadn't trained," he added grimly. "And she cried."

"She cried?" Natalie echoed.

"A lot. Every time she couldn't find something." He ground his teeth.

"Every time you yelled at her?" Natalie guessed.

"I didn't yell. I was very polite."

She bet he was. Icy politeness from Christo Savas would be far worse than being yelled at. "And she left?" Natalie guessed.

He shook his head. "I sacked her, too. And today they

sent two others, but they're hopeless. I sent them back. And the agency doesn't have anyone else. Not until next week. Lisa can come on Thursday. She knows the office. She's worked with your mother. She's worked with me. But I can't put the office on hold until Thursday. And—" he paused and rolled taut shoulders as if doing so would loosen the tension in them "—I can't tell your mother. She'd come back."

She would, too. Natalie knew it. "She might be glad to," she ventured with a slight smile.

Christo's brows raised. "She would?"

"Yes." Natalie sighed. "But she can't. She needs to be there. To get Grandma through this and capable of being on her own again."

He grimaced. "That's what I thought, why I lied. Why I don't want to call her back. So…do you have someone? Just through Wednesday."

"I'll check," Natalie said.

And there it was again, lighting his face—the heart-stopping grin that had seduced her once before—the drop-dead-gorgeous, Christo-Savas-thinks-you're-wonderful smile.

"Terrific," he said. "Just send her to my office tomorrow morning by eight-thirty. I'll get her up to speed. Thanks."

He knew it was a long shot, asking Natalie to supply a secretary. He didn't want to ask her for anything. He'd been vaguely distracted ever since she'd taken up residence at Laura's place.

Not that he'd seen her—except for when he'd caught a glimpse of her in the window of the apartment when he'd been sanding the bookshelves. But she'd disappeared instantly, as if she had no more desire to see him than he did to see her.

Good, he'd thought. But that had been before he'd run out of office help.

He couldn't believe the agency didn't have anyone else. More likely they just didn't have anyone he wouldn't make cry.

Laura never cried. Laura was as tough—and compassionate—as they came. There was nothing she couldn't handle—not his most difficult clients, not cantankerous judges or demanding opposing counsels, not irate parents or Christo himself when his own mother or father breezed in to complicate his life.

If he'd thought he was doing Laura a favor, offering her the job as his secretary and office manager after her divorce, he soon discovered he was the lucky one.

She made his office run efficiently. She smoothed and soothed everyone she came into contact with. She got them to slow down, think clearly, take a deep breath.

"How do you do that?" he'd asked her more than once.

She'd laughed. "Practice. For twenty-five years I was a wife and mother. You don't forget."

Then she'd told him her daughter was creating an agency of temps who could do the same thing. "South Bay Rent-a-Wife, she's calling it." Laura had laughed and shaken her head.

"Your daughter?" The only daughter he knew was Natalie. The other child, he was sure, was a son.

She nodded. "Natalie. You must have met her the summer she was clerking at Ross and Hoy."

Oh yeah. He'd met Natalie all right. But all he'd done was nod. "She's a lawyer."

"No. She dropped out of law school."

"Dropped out?" He remembered how shocked he'd been at Laura's words. And how guilty he'd felt. She hadn't left because of him, had she?

"She always wanted to be a lawyer," Laura said. "Was always her daddy's girl. But when Clayton left—" She paused, and he'd thought she was just going to leave it there, but after a moment, she continued. "Well, Natalie decided she didn't want to be like her father after all." She smiled slightly. "She said she'd rather be like me—but get paid for it."

Christo's eyebrows went up. "Paid for it?"

Laura laughed. "She's a savvy girl, my Natalie. She and Sophy, her cousin, tried it themselves first—worked as 'wives.' Now they run the agency and only step in when they have to. But she tells me her 'wives' can do anything I can do."

Now rifling through the filing cabinet of his office looking for papers yesterday's temp was supposed to have filed there, Christo hoped that was true. Otherwise the next four days were going to be a nightmare.

He glanced at his watch. It was almost eight. He started digging through the file cabinet again. He was getting a bit desperate as he wondered where the hell that blasted woman could have put the Duffy file, when he heard the door to the outer office open.

"In here," he bellowed.

He reached the end of the drawer and banged it shut just as his office door opened. "Good," he said without turning. "You can start looking here. I need the Duffy papers."

"Fine."

His head whipped around at the sound of Natalie's voice.

He opened his mouth, but she forestalled him with a steely smile. "Don't—" she warned "—ask me what the hell I'm doing here. You know what I'm doing here. My mother's job."

She shut the door and set her briefcase on the floor by the coat rack, then straightened. "Struck dumb?" she asked wryly when he didn't speak.

Almost. "You're planning on running my office?" he said, narrowing his gaze.

The mere sight of her in a pencil-slim navy skirt and a high-necked white blouse and a trim navy blazer should have called to mind visions of repressed Catholic school-girls. Instead it was playing havoc with his hormones and giving them decidedly inappropriate ideas. Inappropriate ideas were the last thing he needed right now.

"What do you know about office work?" he demanded.

"I run one," she said. "And I've worked in a law office. And I know my mother. Besides, we don't have anyone else who can do it. So unless you've conjured someone up in the meantime…" She let her voice trail off, inviting him to suggest an alternative.

He didn't have one.

"And you're right," she said. "I don't want you calling my mother."

Their gazes met, clashed. There was a challenge in hers that defied him to argue. He wanted to argue. He wanted her gone, because besides the challenge, that damnable sizzle was there, too. His jaw tightened. He cracked his knuckles.

But before he could figure out an alternative, the phone on the desk rang.

Natalie was closer to it than he was, also faster off the mark. She picked it up.

"Savas Law Office," she said, in a
warm and professional. "Yes," she sai
be happy to. I'm with Mr. Savas righ
moment and I'll have a look at the appo
we can set something up."

She put the phone on hold, set it down,
and looked at Christo. "Unless you'd like
Even her eyebrows were challenging him.

He sucked his teeth. "Be my guest," he
"Just don't cry. I've got a case to prepare."

It was going to be a salutary experience. Four days o
with Christo Savas and she'd be well and truly ove
At least that's what Natalie had been telling
e she hadn't been able to come up with an alter
phy's, "Well, then, I guess you'll have to d
r to whom they were going to send to work for
ldn't

do it!" she'd protested, aghast.

. Her just past six, having spent most of las
a trial h her files looking for a suitable temp
a few who might have some of the
w, was m were already on other jobs. And
h a standout that it made sense to

r Laura. in would be able to think of some-
all, one o could do the job in her mother's
mother, —besides suggesting Natalie do
g. Laura
s the hard ed again.
her bell.
er end of the line. "Why not?
sh on him?"

S
fatu
like
the

I
c

ophy was the one person Natalie had admitted her in-
ation to. And unfortunately her cousin had a memory
an elephant. Thank heavens, she'd never confessed to
mortification in Christo's bedroom.

"I do not have a crush on him," she said firmly. "Once
did. Yes, I admit that. But that was years ago. I was a
hild then."

"So," Sophy said airily. "No problem."

Problem. But she wasn't going to get anywhere arguing
with Sophy. "I'll see what I can come up with," she'd said.

"You know what you have to do," Sophy responded. "I
won't bother you today." And she'd rung off.

Even after Sophy had hung up, Natalie had tried to
come up with alternatives. But short of calling her mother
and telling her the problem, she didn't see one. It was an
indication of how badly she didn't want to do it that once
she actually picked up the phone and began to punch in her
mother's number.

But before she finished, she hung up again. She cou
be that selfish.

Not that her mother wouldn't want to come home
phone call had made it clear just how much of
Grandma Kelling was.

But Laura's duty, as she perceived it, Natalie kne
to be there for her no matter how irritating it was.

Just as her own duty was to step in and take over fo
Her sense of familial love and responsibility was, afte
of the moral tenets Natalie most admired about he
one her father had turned out to be notoriously lackin
never hesitated to do the right thing even when it wa
thing—like putting up with Grandma Kelling and

Like working for Christo Savas.

And so Natalie had dragged herself off to the shower, washed and dried her hair, put on a tailored, professional navy-blue skirt and white blouse, then added a matching navy blazer for good measure. It was armor, and she knew it. But she felt as if she were heading into battle.

Then, shortly before eight, she'd rung Sophy again.

"I'm going," she said without preamble.

"Of course." There was the sound of satisfaction in Sophy's voice. "I knew you would."

Natalie had known she would, too.

And she was determined to begin as she meant to go on—as the consummate professional. So she shut the door on Christo, leaving him to the files in his office while she went out to the reception area to finish the call she'd taken and schedule the appointment required.

It wasn't difficult to step into her mother's shoes. She understood the way her mother did things, her work-flow pattern as it were, the process she used to get things done.

Laura had never done things haphazardly as a wife and mother. She wasn't rigid, but in the Ross household there had always been a place for things, and things were always in their place.

So it was no trouble now for Natalie to open the middle left-hand drawer of her mother's desk and find the appointment book right where she expected it would be. She ran her eyes down Christo's appointments for the next week, understood quickly the general pattern of his days, picked up the phone, and offered the caller three possible times.

She wrote the client's choice in the book, hung up the phone and realized that Christo was standing in the door to his office staring at her.

"What?" she said.

He shook his head. "Three out of four of them couldn't find the appointment book. Two of them said it should be on the computer."

"My mother wouldn't keep the primary schedule on the computer."

"I know." He rocked back and forth on his heels. For a moment he didn't say anything else. Then he said, "Suppose you find the Duffy file then."

"Did my mother file it?" Natalie asked.

He shrugged. "God knows."

Life in the office got almost instantly better—and simultaneously worse.

It was better in the sense that Christo didn't have to quit what he was doing to rescue and detraumatize young clients whom Tuesday's martinet had pointed to chairs, fixed with a steely stare and commanded, "Sit there and don't move."

Natalie found the books and puzzles and toys her mother kept in the cabinet, and if a parent with children or a child he was representing had to wait for him, she saw that they were calm and engaged until Christo could see them.

She fielded phone calls without interrupting him. She took legible notes and reported conversations accurately. It took her a while to find the Duffy file—because it hadn't been filed at all, but had been shuffled in with another case's pre-trial motions.

When he was terse and demanding, which admittedly he sometimes was, she didn't take it personally and burst into tears. She simply did what needed to be done. And more. When he missed lunch to attend a meeting, for example, he found a sandwich sitting on his desk when he got back.

As far as Christo could tell, by the end of the afternoon

Natalie was up to speed and every bit as capable as her mother at juggling three opposing counsels, two cranky judges, one school social worker and, for all he knew, a partridge in a pear tree.

Workwise, then, Natalie Ross was everything he could ask for—her work wasn't a problem at all.

Seeing her was.

When he opened the door to his office that afternoon, he felt an instant punch in the gut seeing Natalie at Laura's desk. Her mother was an attractive woman, but Natalie was beautiful. And there was a light and a vitality about Natalie that took her beauty to a whole different level. She was smiling up at Madeleine Dirksen, one of his weepier clients, while at the same time bouncing Madeleine's two-year-old on her knee.

"You can come in now," he said to Madeleine.

"I'll keep Jacob for you," Natalie offered.

Madeleine gave her a grateful smile. "Would you mind?"

"Not at all," Natalie assured her and slanted a quick glance in Christo's direction. "He can help me file."

Christo ushered Madeleine into his office, fully expecting to hear Jacob start howling or, before long, bookcases crashing. But no untoward sounds reached his ears. And when he and Madeleine emerged an hour later it was to find Natalie with the phone tucked between her ear and her shoulder while she scribbled notes with one hand and kept the other wrapped around Jacob who, thumb in his mouth, was sound asleep on her lap.

Madeleine blinked back her tears and gave her a wobbly wet smile. "Ah, wonderful."

"He is," Natalie agreed. "I'll carry him out to your car if you'd like. That way he may not wake up."

When she got back she had a question about one of the letters he'd wanted typed. "Here," she said. "This doesn't make sense to me." She rattled off some of his legalese, pointing at it on the computer screen.

He crossed the room to have a look, and discovered that if the sight of Natalie rattled him, breathing in the scent of her distracted the hell out of him.

As he leaned over her shoulder to have a look at what she didn't understand, he caught the scent of some wild-flowery sort of shampoo. Not a strong scent; it was barely evident, in fact. He stepped closer, breathed deeper. Shut his eyes.

"Did you leave a word out?" Natalie turned her head to look up at him so their faces were scant inches apart.

Christo jumped back. "What? What word?"

"I don't know, do I?" she said with some aspersion. "You're the one who's writing the letter."

"Er." He had to step closer then to try to make sense of his words on the screen, to see what he'd been saying, to recapture his train of thought. And he caught another whiff of wildflowers. He stiffened and held his breath.

Natalie turned once more, her brows drawn together. "Are you catching a cold?"

"What?"

"You're sniffling. Do you have allergies?"

"No, damn it. I don't have allergies." He spun away and stalked back into his office. "Forget it. I'll do it tomorrow."

"We're working tomorrow?"

"Not you. Me." He'd need his Saturday morning in the office just to catch up from the week's earlier disasters— not to mention from proximity to Natalie.

He shut the door, sank into his chair and pinched the

bridge of his nose. Why the hell had he ever asked her to find him a secretary?

Why the hell had she agreed to do it?

He knew the answers. Or at least the acceptable ones.

But three more days of this?

Be careful what you wish for, his Brazilian grandmother always used to tell him.

Now he really understood exactly what she meant.

"You're still here." The words were more accusation than question. Christo, arms braced on either side of the open doorway, collar unbuttoned, tie loose, was glowering at her as if she were doing something wrong. "It's past six o'clock."

Natalie shrugged. "I still had work to do." She forbore pointing out that he was still here, too. "My mother taught me not to leave things undone." She picked up the last of the papers she was filing and concentrated on finding the proper folder in the drawer, not allowing herself to look again at the man across the room.

The theory behind vaccinations—the one that had brought her here to work for him today—was that if you introduced a small dose of something dire into your system, you would develop antibodies that would help you resist the Big Bad Real Thing.

Good idea for resisting polio and smallpox and influenza. It didn't help with resisting Christo Savas one bit.

A little exposure to Christo simply made her want more. And the more chance she had to look at him, the more her eyes tried to follow his every move. The more he demanded, the more she was determined to prove equal to the task. And as he shoved away from the door and came toward her, she found herself leaning toward him.

God, was gravity against her, too?

Certainly her own inclinations were. Far from getting over him, she was as attracted as ever. Possibly more, because Christo the litigator had been a brilliant incisive attractive man. But this Christo, who took time with weeping women and who had spent half an hour putting a puzzle together with a shy little girl before he ever got her to say a word—this Christo was even more appealing. He was kind, he was compassionate. He was caring. He was human.

He was everything she'd once believed him to be—except available to fall in love with.

"I'm going now," she said, slipping the last file into the correct folder and shutting the drawer with a firm push. She plucked her blazer off the coat rack and put it on, feeling a sudden need for armor again under the intensity of his hooded gaze. "You don't want me to come in tomorrow?"

"No."

That was certainly clear enough. "Right." She picked up her briefcase. "Well, I'll see you Monday, then." She opened the door.

"Natalie." Her name on his lips stopped her in her tracks. She looked back.

He sucked in a breath. "Your mother would be proud."

She smiled faintly. "I hope so."

She left quickly, closing the door behind her. Three years ago she thought she'd made the biggest mistake of her life. Today—coming to work for Christo—she wondered if she might have made a bigger one.

Saturdays were catch-up day.

Christo didn't work at his office every Saturday. But when things piled up during the week and he needed quiet time to work out his arguments, to think outside the box and get new perspectives on cases, he headed for his office.

There were no clients demanding attention on Saturdays. There were no judges or other attorneys calling, and there were no household chores to distract him.

Saturday at the office was, hands-down, the best day and the best place for productive, intense, focused work.

Or it had been until now.

Now, the minute he walked in the door he caught a hint of Natalie's elusive wildflower shampoo. Her handwriting was on a note on the top of his pile of things-to-do. He found himself prowling through his file drawers looking into folders she'd filed, studying notes she'd made. Ostensibly it was because he needed the information.

But he couldn't quite lie to himself well enough to believe it didn't have something to do with his preoccupation with Natalie.

He shut the file drawer and went back to his desk, but he didn't sit down. He paced the length of his office and asked himself, not for the first time, what the hell it was about Natalie that got under his skin?

Or was it simply that she was the one who'd got away?

She didn't *get away,* he reminded himself irritably. She'd turned up in his bed and he'd effectively tossed her out. End of story.

Except it wasn't the end of the story. And however hard he tried to concentrate on the argument he was trying to write, memories of Natalie kept niggling in his brain.

Instead of an annoyance it was a relief when his cell phone rang to distract him. And when he saw the number calling his mood lightened at once. *"Avó!"*

"Ah, Christo. I miss you."

The sound of his Brazilian grandmother's voice could always make him smile. He missed her, too. "What's up?"

She was a dynamo, his grandmother, always involved in a hundred different things. He tipped back in his chair now and put his feet on the desk, letting her voice carry him back to the place she called home. She told him about the crops—it was a farm as well as an estate of note these days. She told him all about her neighbors and the extended family and her many bridge games. She kept him up to date on where his father was.

"In Buenos Aires this week," she said. "Last week in Paris."

Par for the course as far as Christo was concerned. Xantiago Azevedo, whom he'd never called Dad or Papa or anything other than Xanti, the name on the back of his father's soccer shirt, had been on the move all of Christo's life.

He hadn't even met his father until he was nearly six. And then it had been a surprise to both of them.

Xanti had come to play in a match in L.A., and he'd had a night to kill before his plane left for Sao Paulo the next day. At loose ends, he'd apparently decided to look up an old flame. Probably, Christo realized later, he had decided to see if Aurora Savas wanted a roll in the hay for old time's sake.

Xanti hadn't actually said that in so many words—not that Christo would have understood them at the time if he had—but he'd definitely blinked in surprise when the door had been opened by a boy who looked just like him.

"Who're you?" Xanti had demanded.

Before Christo could say more than his first name, his mother had come up behind him. "Meet your son, Xanti," she'd said to his dumbstruck father. "Want to take him home with you for the summer?"

Surprisingly enough, Xanti had.

But not before he'd married Aurora.

"Of course, we will marry," he'd said, adding with the foolish nobility Xanti generally approached things with in the short run, "It is my duty."

Maybe. But his commitment to it didn't last. It was the long run Xanti was never able to handle, which is why the whirlwind marriage had lasted barely two months.

Still, it had given Christo a grandmother who loved him and a home away from home in Brazil. Widowed Lucia Azevedo had welcomed her only grandchild with open arms. With her husband deceased and Xanti, her only child, jetting around the world playing soccer and sleeping with women, this unexpected grandchild quickly became the light of her life.

And Christo, after a week of determined indifference, found his resolve undermined by Avó's equally determined love. Her gentle smiles and calm acceptance undid his resolution to remain aloof from this new world he'd been thrust into—a world in which he didn't even speak the language.

"No matter," Avó had said. "We will learn each other."

Teach, she'd meant. But "learn each other" was exactly what they'd done. Now, twenty-six years later, Christo spoke with her in the same mixture of English and Portuguese that they'd come to then.

"*'Stas bem?*" he asked her. "Are you okay?" because she'd had fainting spells recently.

"*Sim, sim. Muito bem. Perfeita.*" She dismissed his concerns. "And you? Have you met the girl yet?"

Abruptly the idyll was over and a vision of Natalie popped back into his head.

He sat up and jerked his feet off the desk. "No."

Ordinarily he brushed off the question with a laugh. It wasn't as if she didn't regularly ask him.

Having given up on Xanti ever settling down—though he'd been with the same woman, Katia, for almost a year now—Lucia had made it clear she was counting on Christo to marry and settle down and give her babies to dote on.

He'd never told her he had no intention of marrying because it would upset her. She would think it was her fault, that she hadn't taught him well enough about love and family and the value of marriage. But today he felt edgier than he usually did.

And his grandmother picked up on it. "You are looking though, *sim?*"

"I—" *Damn it, no.* And he didn't intend to.

"I had a good marriage with your grandfather," she reminded him. "If he had lived, maybe Xanti—" And then her voice trailed off. "No matter," she said briskly after a moment. "Xanti is who he is. But you—you will find her, Christo," she assured him, her voice strong again. "Or I will find her for you."

Since he'd turned thirty, two years ago, she'd been offering to do that regularly.

"Não é necessário," he assured her again now.

"Alicia, she would be good for you. She is going to be a lawyer, too," his grandmother went on as if she hadn't heard. "So you will have something to talk about."

Christo let her talk. He didn't discourage her ever. He'd tried that, but it made her despondent and led to despairing comments like, "What have I done wrong? It's not just your father who can't settle down. Now you, too!"

"You want to meet her?" his grandmother asked hopefully.

Not really. "I'm busy," Christo said. "I don't know

when I'll be back to Brazil." He was in no hurry to go down for a visit if Avó was planning to set him up with dates when he did.

"*Sim,* I know." She sounded sad now. "It has been a year."

"I'll get there, I promise."

"As Xanti promises."

He heard a weary resignation in her tone. Christo's jaw tightened. "Yes, but I keep mine," he reminded her.

"I know you do." Her voice was gentle. "So you will come."

"I will," Christo said firmly. "Before Christmas. I'll call you in a couple of weeks and we can talk about it."

"Of course we can. You are my favorite grandson." It was what she always said.

"I'm your only grandson," he reminded her with a grin.

"That is so," she agreed. "I love you, my Christo."

"You, too. *Tchau, 'Vó. Beijos.*"

He hung up, slumped in his chair and tipped his head back. Now visions of his doting grandmother overlaid those of Natalie in his mind. Avó would like Natalie. Natalie would like his grandmother as well.

It didn't bear thinking about.

CHAPTER THREE

THERE were no hot looks from Christo on Monday morning. No glances that lingered. No politeness even.

Well, Natalie supposed he was polite enough. But he was absolutely businesslike, curt and remote every time he spoke to her. The intense awareness she'd felt on Friday was more like a determined deep freeze today. He didn't even meet her eyes, but looked out the window all the time he was giving her instructions.

She remembered her mother saying more than once, "Christo is such a pleasure to work for. He's always so even-tempered."

Even-tempered, as in his range of emotions went from stern to dour? He smiled enough at his clients. But he scarcely looked at her.

He wouldn't even take the time after his nine-thirty appointment left to come and look at a scan of a handwritten document she had up on the computer screen.

"You can figure it out," he said curtly and stayed at his desk, not looking up as he flipped through papers and sorted them into folders. Natalie knew he had two pre-trial conferences in L.A. in the afternoon. She supposed he was preoccupied with them.

He saw two more clients, then came out of his office shortly before one. "I won't be back until late." He was shrugging into his suit coat and his tie was once more neatly knotted, his hair just combed.

"Anything else I should do while you're gone?" Natalie asked.

"Take a lunch break."

She blinked.

"You didn't on Friday. You went out and grabbed sandwiches." It sounded more like an accusation than a comment. "So today, go eat. I won't be back until late," he went on. "So I don't need you bringing me sandwiches."

So the sandwich had offended him, had it? Why? Had it made him think she was making another bid for attention? As if! She had simply done what she knew her mother would have done.

But she didn't say that. She gave a light shrug, as if it didn't matter one way or the other to her. It didn't. It really didn't.

Christo opened the door, then looked back over his shoulder. "You don't need to stay late, either."

Natalie didn't even deign to reply to that.

She would stay late if she had work to finish. If she didn't, she'd leave. And he could take his handsome face and his bloodymindedness and go stuff them both where they'd do some good.

"Whatever you say, boss," she muttered. But he was gone and didn't hear her.

Just as well. She finished the letter she was working on, then at quarter past one, took her lunch break, as ordered. She didn't leave the office, but ate her tuna fish sandwich sitting at her mother's desk. She did, however, spend the time catching up on her own work for Rent-a-Wife.

Sophy had done the scheduling this week, but Natalie still had the billing to do. If Mr. Stickler Savas wanted everything in businesslike boxes from here on out, that was fine with her. She'd do her work now and start back on his after lunch.

Her brother Dan called to ask if she would like his daughter Jamii to come for the weekend. "Kelly and I got invited to visit a high-school friend of hers in Sausalito. They live on a houseboat. We thought it would be cool. But if you'd rather not…"

"No, I'd like it," Natalie said. Her eight-year-old niece would be a welcome distraction from the man who was currently occupying most every waking thought—to no avail.

"Great!" Dan was delighted. "We'll drop her off after work on Friday and pick her up before dinner on Sunday. You can come out to dinner with us."

"Sounds good."

"If Kelly has anything she wants to add, I'll have her call you."

He rang off and, after a quick glance at her watch that showed she still had ten minutes of Rent-a-Wife time, she went back to work.

Immediately the office phone rang.

She could have let the answering machine get it, she thought grimly even as she reached to pick it up. But however annoying Christo was being, she couldn't inconvenience his clients that way.

"Savas Law Office."

"Thank God you're there. I need you to bring me a folder."

No question who it was. Natalie nearly choked on her tuna-fish.

"It's in my office. It has to be," he went on. "I spent an

hour Saturday morning making sure I had all of it in one place after those temps screwed things up." He sounded as though he wanted to strangle someone. So much for Mr. Cool-and-Remote.

"Which folder?"

"Eamon Duffy's. His is the second of the two conferences I have this afternoon. And his original birth certificate, the custody agreement and the divorce decree aren't here."

"Can't the judge just pull them up on the computer?"

"They're from out of state. I don't know where the hell they are! Did you misfile them?"

"Would I know if I had?" Natalie countered acerbically.

"Sorry," he muttered. But he didn't sound sorry. He sounded at the end of his rope.

"I'll look," Natalie was already heading into his office.

"You'll have to tear the place apart."

"Not likely," Natalie said, seeing them on the tabletop under the mirror where he'd probably set them when he'd straightened his tie and combed his hair. "Where are you?"

"You found them?"

"Yes. Where are you?"

He gave her the address and directions to the court building. He was waiting when she got there and took the folder gratefully. He even looked at her. And it was back— the electricity. She could feel it. It was almost a relief—as if the world had righted itself.

"Need anything else?" she asked, her tone gently mocking, when she handed it to him. "A sandwich perhaps?"

His mouth twisted wryly.

She shrugged and was turning to leave when his voice halted her.

"Natalie."

She glanced back, met his gaze. Oh, God, yes, you could light the whole city of Los Angeles with the electricity now. "Hmm?"

"Thanks."

Some things, Natalie decided, were just not a good idea.

One of them had been agreeing to work for Christo. Not that she didn't enjoy it. She did. Too much. She liked the work, liked interacting with many of his clients, liked the variety and the challenge.

Liked being able to look up or across the room and see Christo himself.

That she probably relished more than anything else. But it wasn't the salutary experience she'd hoped it would be—or at least not salutary in the way she'd hoped. It wasn't helping her get over him at all. In fact, by Wednesday, her last day in the office, she knew she needed to get out.

It wasn't that she was afraid she would disgrace herself again. It was how badly she wanted to.

Well, not really to disgrace herself. But she did want Christo Savas with a deep, profound, gut-level desire unlike any she'd ever known. And she shouldn't.

It was pathetic. *She* was pathetic, and she knew it.

"Get over it," she told herself. "You've been down this road before."

So she tried. But she kept looking up to feast her eyes on him every time he came into the reception area. She welcomed every opportunity to go into his office when he was there.

She found herself memorizing the way his brows drew together when he was studying an argument and how he tapped his pen against his teeth when he was reading. She had an image in her mind of the way he always tilted his head and listened so intently when one of his clients was speaking, and how he always crouched down so he was on eye level with the children as he was doing now with eight-year-old Derek Hartman who was showing Christo baseball cards instead of talking about his parents' divorce.

She wondered what he'd be like with children of his own. And the vision of Christo with little green-eyed boys and dark-haired girls pierced so sharply that she had to catch her breath.

"Don't," she said sharply.

Christo, just straightening up to take Derek into the conference room, looked around at her. "Did you say something?"

"No—" her cheeks were burning "—I just—no. Never mind. Made a mistake." She waved in the general direction of the letter she was supposed to be typing. "Just... muttering."

He gave her an odd look, then shrugged. "What are you doing tonight?"

Her gaze jerked up. Her heart kicked over. "What?"

"I've got the shelves ready. Can I come up and put them in?"

"Oh." Deflated and annoyed at feeling deflated, she shrugged. "Sure. Of course."

He knocked. And knocked again.

She didn't answer the door.

It was just past seven. He didn't know what time she'd left the office because he'd been on a conference call between five and six. When he'd finished, though, and come out of his office, she was already gone.

Her car was in the garage. So she should be home. Though, he supposed, she could have walked up to the shops on Manhattan Avenue.

Or she might be on a date.

He knocked again. Louder. "Natalie!"

No answer. He hadn't seen anyone come and pick her up. But then, he hadn't spent the last hour watching her door, had he? He had better things to do. Besides, she'd told him he could come tonight.

But she hadn't said she'd be here, he reminded himself.

Well, fine. She knew he had a key. He'd let himself in. He went back home and got it, then when one last knock got no reply, he opened the door and went in.

The apartment might be Laura's, but it had Natalie's mark on it now. That was her laundry folded in neat piles on the kitchen table. Her colorful T-shirts and scoop-necked tops, her shorts and capris, her skimpy equally colorful underwear.

He didn't need to be thinking about Natalie's underwear. He still remembered the pink camisole top she'd worn the night he'd found her in his bed. Still—

He shoved the memory away and began hauling in the shelves. Herbie, ever curious, followed him, wove between his feet, tripping him and meowing at the same time.

"Didn't she feed you?" Christo asked him.

But he could see that Herbie still had a bit of food in his bowl. She'd obviously been home. And then he saw her open day planner by the coffeemaker. In Natalie's hand-writing, it said, Scott 6:30.

So—his jaw tightened—*a date, after all.*

No matter. He could work faster without her interference. He had plenty of interference with Herbie before the cat got bored and decided Christo wasn't going to provide any food. Then Herbie curled up beside Natalie's CDs on the cabinet under the window, and Christo began putting the bookcases together.

He liked working with his hands, liked the feel of the wood beneath his fingers, liked fitting things together and making something useful. Doing that was a good counterpoint to the thinking he had to do for his legal work. Often as he worked, his mind did the same, exploring possibilities, considering options, framing and reframing arguments, asking himself questions.

Like, who the hell was Scott?

He put on the wood glue and fitted the back to the side.

And why hadn't she ever mentioned him?

He was meticulous with his work, drilling and gluing and countersinking the screws. It was the sort of work that usually settled his mind. All he could think right now was he could have used another pair of hands.

It was past nine when Natalie finally appeared. "Oh," she said when she pushed open the door and found him kneeling in the living room as he put the blind screws into the back of the first bookcase. "You're still here."

"Imagine that."

"What's wrong?"

"Nothing's wrong," he said sharply. "Give me a hand here. Unless you're worried about getting your clothes dirty."

She wasn't wearing the gray skirt and blazer with the black blouse she'd worn to the office. Not dressing for success tonight, then. She had on a casual flowered skirt in a sort of batik print with a rust-colored top that brought out the red in her hair. Probably the way Scott preferred it.

She hesitated. "I will. But let me change," she said. "I only have so many work clothes."

Christo's eyes widened. "Work?"

"I went to dinner with a new client tonight."

Scott at six-thirty was a client? "Dressed like that?"

She blinked in surprise, then realized what he expected to see in the way of work clothes. "I'm not a lawyer," she reminded him.

His teeth set. He studied her clothing. "And that's what wives wear?"

She shrugged. "More or less. Less tailored than lawyers. More casual and approachable, but still businesslike."

"Just," he muttered.

"What?"

"Nothing. Get changed and come give me a hand here."

It should have been easier with the two of them working. It wasn't.

The second pair of hands was helpful. But the way they bumped into each other was not.

Nor was the faceful of her hair he seemed to get every time he moved close. Damn it, Natalie! But he didn't say it. Just breathed it in. Breathed the scent of her—and felt that plaguing desire grow.

It made him want to do more than brush an arm against her. It made him want to reach out and pull her into his arms.

She shifted to get a better grip on the bookcase as they were moving it and her breasts brushed against his arm.

His breath hissed between his teeth. "Damn it. I said move." He grunted.

"I am."

"Not that way!" She turned and he got her hair in his face again. "Are you trying to drive me nuts?"

Her shoulders stiffened. She looked at him, confused. "Drive you nuts?"

His jaw worked. "All that shifting, twisting, turning—"

"I was trying to help! You said to move."

"To move. Not rub against me!"

Her mouth formed an astonished *O*. Then it twitched shut and he saw a sudden twinkle in her eye. "Am I threatening your virtue, Mr. Savas?" she asked mockingly. Then she added more seriously, "I didn't think I could."

He gritted his teeth. "Think again."

Natalie blinked. "You're kidding." She sounded genuinely surprised.

He supposed he should be glad, happy that she hadn't noticed. But all he could do was glare at her. "What? You think I'm immune?"

"You certainly were last time!"

"The hell I was!"

She stared at him, shocked. "You sent me away."

"You were a kid!"

"I was twenty-two!"

"Too young for me. Too innocent," he added pointedly. "And you worked with me."

"Not when I came here. I had finished at Ross and Hoy earlier that week. I know the rules. I know about impropriety."

"You don't know a damn thing about impropriety," he told her flatly. "And if I had taken you up on your offer, that wouldn't have been the end of it. Would it?"

"What do you mean?"

"You would have wanted to get married."

"Married?" There was a hectic flush on her cheeks.

"You would have." He flung the accusation at her. It was

no secret. She'd been that kind of girl. "If I'd slept with you—had sex with you—" he made it as blunt as he could "—you wouldn't have been willing just to walk away, would you?"

She opened her mouth, but no words came out. She didn't need to say them. He already knew.

"No, you wouldn't. You'd have wanted a relationship. You and me. Happily ever after. *Married.*" He spat the word at her, daring her to dispute it.

Natalie ran her tongue over her lips, still silent, her eyes spearing him.

He gritted his teeth. "You wouldn't have wanted a one-night fling, Natalie. You'd have wanted it all."

"Yes, I would have," she said at last, her voice quiet but steady. "What's wrong with that?"

Christo felt instantly justified. "It's foolishness. It creates false expectations. It does more harm than good."

"Does it?" She didn't sound convinced.

"Damn it, yes, it does! Look at your parents! Look at mine. You don't know them," he said, "but take it from me, they were a disaster together."

"I'm sorry."

He didn't want her sorrow. Or her pity. Or anything else. The only thing he wanted, heaven help him, was her.

He shook his head, turned away. And damned if she didn't put a hand on his arm. He jerked away. "Don't."

But she persisted, wrapped her fingers around his forearm, nails digging lightly into his flesh as she tugged him around to make him look at her. "Christo."

"No."

"Yes."

It was that single quiet insistent word that undermined

his resolve. He turned toward her, anguished. "You don't know what you're saying. You're going to be sorry."

Mutely she shook her head, looking up at him, eyes brimming with emotion. "I appreciate what you did three years ago." She offered him a ghost of a smile. "Now that I know why you did it. But I'm not the girl I was then. You don't have to protect me anymore, Christo."

His jaw tightened. "Right. So you're going to protect yourself?" He didn't see how.

She shrugged. "I'm a big girl. I'm a grown-up. I was grown up then, but foolish perhaps. Maybe I still am," she acknowledged. "But that's my problem, not yours." Her hand slid up his arm, touched his cheek.

And damn it, he couldn't help turning his face so that his lips touched her palm. He shut his eyes and took a desperate breath. He felt as if he was standing on the edge of a cliff, the slightest movement capable of blowing him right over.

"Christo." Her voice was soft, close enough that he could feel the words on his skin. Then closer still. Her lips traced his jawline.

Christo had as much willpower as the next man. More than most, probably. But there were limits. He'd met his.

And he couldn't fight it any longer. His arms wrapped around her. His own lips sought her mouth, took it in a desperate move, one his body had been wanting to make for days. One his mind could no longer resist.

Maybe he'd have had a burst of sanity—if she'd panicked, if she'd shown the slightest resistance, if she hadn't slid her arms around him and held him tight, if he hadn't felt her heart thunder in rhythm with his own, if her mouth hadn't been as eager as his.

But she was as eager as he was. And as they kissed, as his hands roamed her back, he wondered how he had resisted temptation so long.

The feel of her hands on him was sweet torture. Fingers slipped under his shirt and walked up his spine. He arched his back and felt the exquisite pressure of his erection pressing against her belly.

Natalie felt it, too. Had to. Had to know how much he wanted her.

"Nat." His voice was low and thick with his need for her. Saying her name was as much of a warning as he was capable of. That and stillness. One last moment of gripping her upper arms, holding her motionless. He felt a shudder run through him—the last of his willpower gone.

Her lips touched his. "Love me, Christo."

It wasn't love. He wanted to say that to her, but the words wouldn't come.

Only the kisses came. Hungry desperate kisses. The taste of her was making him crazy. He steered her toward the sofa, needed to hold her, to lie with her.

"Not here," she whispered. And taking his hand, she led the way into the small guest room where she was staying. The bed was only a single size. It didn't matter. They wouldn't need more.

She had dropped the clothes she'd worn to her meeting on the bed when she'd changed. Now she scooped them off and put them on the chair. Then she turned back to him with a smile and drew him down with her, ran her hands up under his shirt, her fingers cool on his heated flesh.

And Christo touched her with a reverence that surprised him. Sex was recreation. It was meeting physical needs. But holding Natalie in his arms didn't feel like recreation.

And sliding his hands up her sides and cupping her breasts in his hands didn't feel like the same simple assuaging of physical needs.

He was learning the joy of touching her. Watching her face to see the expressions that passed over it. As he lay down beside her and wrapped her in his arms, she moved closer so that their knees touched, their hips bumped, her lips grazed the line of his jaw and chin. Christo nuzzled her hair, breathing deeply now, allowing himself to relish the scent of it—of her.

Minutes ago he'd resisted, fought off the desire it provoked, tried in vain to remain indifferent to her.

But that was then. And now?

Now he didn't think. He didn't analyze. He didn't argue pro or con. He simply savored. And wanted more.

He took it, too, because Natalie encouraged him. She made soft sounds that made his heart beat faster, made him want to hear more, feel more, taste more.

He stroked her silken skin beneath her shirt. It was so smooth, so warm, it seemed to encourage the glide of his fingers. Then he shoved himself up to kneel beside her and draw her shirt up. He tugged it over her head, then bent to press his lips to her collarbone, and nibble his way down between her breasts. His hands framed her rib cage and he kissed his way down to her navel.

"Christo!" Her eyes were dark and wide, her lips formed a soft *O* at his touch. And then she skimmed his shirt over his head as well and rose to kiss his chest and run her fingers over his pectoral muscles.

It was a dance of fingers and lips. Touches and nibbles, light friction, gentle stroking. And every one stoked the fire building within.

He dispensed with her bra then knelt between her knees and cupped her breasts in his palms. And she watched him, unblinking, her lower lip caught in her teeth, her breath coming in soft thready whispers.

With his fingers he traced the aureoles around taut nipples, then bent his head and laved each one in turn, making her shiver and shift beneath him. And the look on her face made him as eager for her as she was for him.

He pulled back and hooked his thumbs inside the waistband of her shorts when she lifted her hips, slid them down her legs and tossed them away. Only a scrap of pale-blue cotton and lace covered her now.

"Christo." She reached for his zip, and with fumbling fingers he yanked it down and shed his jeans, kicking them aside, then peeled off his boxers as well, sucking in his breath as the cool night air coming through the window hit his heated bare flesh.

He would have bared her, too, then, but she reached out a hand and touched him lightly, stroked the length of him, made him clench his teeth and suck in a sharp breath. It hissed through his teeth and she said, "Are you all right?"

"No. I'm going to lose it completely in half a second if you do that again. Don't. Touch."

Her eyes widened as she jerked her hand away. "Ever?"

He laughed, a strained laugh, one that revealed to him, if not to her, just how tenuous a grip he had on his control. "No. Just now. I want—I want to take it slow and that's…not going to happen."

He skimmed the lacy panties down her legs and then slid trembling fingers back up the length of them, touched her, teased her, probed her gently.

Now Natalie sucked in a breath, too. Her hips shifted. Her fingers clenched on the quilt that covered the bed. And Christo moved between her knees, stroking her now, parting her, finding her as ready for him as he was for her.

Then she was grasping his hips and pulling him down to her, her need as naked as her body as she opened to him.

Naked bodies meant nothing more than pleasure. Naked emotions were something else again. But he couldn't look away. She mesmerized him, made him ache with the need of her.

He couldn't turn back now. Couldn't resist the pull to join his body to hers.

He slid in, took her. Gave himself over to the need that surged within him, and tried to give Natalie the satisfaction that she was giving him.

She was so hot, so tight. So right.

He wanted the feeling to last forever. Wanted desperately to slow it down, hang onto it, to let it build and ease and build again, to make it grow as well inside her.

But Natalie thwarted his best intentions with intentions of her own. She moved against him, rocked her hips, drew him deeper, arched her back and clenched around him.

"Now," she whispered, her fingers digging into his buttocks, her heels hard against the backs of his thighs. They moved together, eager and desperate until together they tipped over the edge into oblivion.

Spent, shattered, Christo could barely lift his head. His heart thundered. He pressed a kiss to her cheek, to her lips, then pulled back enough to look down at her, to feel sanity returning, but what else he wasn't sure.

Natalie stared up at him, speechless, her gaze unreadable.

And Christo felt a stab of anxiety. Of doubt. He stroked her cheek with still-trembling fingers. "Are you all right?"

Because she didn't look all right. She looked stunned.

And then, like morning light, a smile dawned. Slowly at first, touching her lips, then suffusing her whole face. She loosed her hands that were locked around his back and brought them up to frame his face.

"I don't think *all right* really covers it," she said. And then she raised up to press her lips to his.

They loved again that night.

Slow and easy the second time, as they let their touches linger, she and Christo learned each other's bodies, each other's needs, each other's desires. But slow and easy was no less shattering than fast and desperate.

Nor was lying in the narrow bed and watching Christo sleep afterwards.

"I'll go," he'd said only moments after they'd spent themselves the last time. He was lying on his side, his body curved around hers, his arm slung possessively across her waist, holding her against him. And she had felt the whisper of his words against her ear.

She hadn't moved then. She'd simply held onto the moment, reliving the night from its unpromising beginning to this, marveling at the change.

Who'd have thought?

After a while she realized that he hadn't moved. His hold on her hand had loosened, his breathing had slowed. He was sleeping.

With exquisite care and deliberation, Natalie shifted her body. There wasn't much room. She hugged the edge of the bed as she rolled onto her back, still in his embrace, then turned just enough to face him, wanting to see him, to study his features in the dim light that spilled in through the window from the street.

She had never seen Christo unguarded before. Never seen him without armor. She didn't mean clothes, though of course his lack of them allowed her to learn that part of him as well. It could have made him vulnerable.

But it didn't. Christo had a strong body, lean but well-muscled, with hard ropy arms, a flat abdomen, strong thighs. He didn't look like a man who went to meetings and wrote arguments all day. It reminded her that that was only a part of who he was.

He was also the man who slept next to her, his features softened slightly by sleep. His jaw was relaxed now, his lips slightly parted. The hard, often wary green eyes were hidden beneath long-lashed lids. He looked gentler. A bit more like the man she'd dreamed of finding beneath the hard tough shell the world saw.

She'd found that man tonight. Against all odds, he'd finally listened to what she'd said.

It was her problem she loved him. Her foolishness, perhaps. She knew the gentleness and vulnerability wouldn't last. She knew the armor, gone now, would come back in the strong light of day.

He would be Christo Savas again, the tough lawyer the world knew.

But she would know this Christo. She would have these memories. She had broken through the armor to the man inside.

And she dared hope—dared believe—that he would find joy in letting her in, in sharing the intimacies they'd shared again. And again.

She lifted a hand and touched his hair. It was both crisp and soft under her fingers. She trailed them down to trace the line of his ear and jaw. She pressed a finger lightly to his lips, felt his breath against it almost like a kiss.

He didn't wake. He only sighed. And smiled the barest of smiles.

Natalie smiled, too, and knew that whatever happened, she would never regret this night. She slid her arm around him and rested her head against his chest. In her ear she could feel the solid strong beat of his heart.

She loved listening to it. Loved being this close to him. Had loved being even closer.

Three years she had waited. But he had been worth waiting for.

"I love you," she whispered and pressed a kiss to his chest. Then she closed her eyes, too, and slept.

In the morning, when she awoke, he was gone.

CHAPTER FOUR

"You look bright," Sophy studied Natalie with un-
abashed interest when she walked into the office the
next morning.

"Glad to be back," Natalie said airily. It was partly the
truth, but not the part that was making it a struggle to keep
the grin off her face. Even though Christo had been gone
when she got up, she hadn't been able to stop smiling.

The memories of the night before had a lot to do with
it. But even more was the note on the dining-room table that
said in Christo's spiky neat writing, "I'll see you tonight."

"Things worked out okay with Christo, then?"

Natalie did a momentary double-take, then realized
Sophy had no way of knowing anything about last night,
that it wasn't what had happened between her and Christo
that her cousin was talking about.

"Um, at work, you mean? Yes. Yes, they did." Natalie
busied herself unpacking her laptop, setting it up, plugging
in the power cord.

Sophy regarded her speculatively. "And what about not
at work?" she ventured after a long moment.

Natalie felt the heat rise in her cheeks. "Fine," she said

shortly. "He's fine." But she didn't meet Sophy's gaze, though she could certainly feel her cousin's curious eyes on her.

Then there was a sharp intake of breath. "You're not telling me something," Sophy said.

"Nothing to tell. I finished work for him yesterday. His old temp is back today."

Sophy didn't say anything.

Natalie looked over at her. Sophy's gaze was narrow, assessing her every move. And clearly detecting the hint of a smile that Natalie couldn't quite hide.

"You did it," Sophy breathed. "Didn't you?" she pressed when Natalie didn't immediately reply.

In fact, Natalie had no intention of replying. She didn't kiss and tell. Or do anything else and tell about it, either.

"I just said he was fine. That's all I said." She fixed a glare on Sophy.

But whatever subtle signs the other woman was reading, she had no doubt. "Wow," she said softly. Then she leaned toward Natalie, her dark eyes gentle and concerned. "So, who changed? Christo? Or you?"

There was no point in pretending she didn't know what Sophy was talking about. But Natalie sat down and booted up her computer before she answered.

Then she said with quiet honesty, "I don't know."

"Oh, dear. You be careful. Those Savas men are hell on hearts."

Sophy knew that better than almost anyone, having been married to one of Christo's cousins briefly a few years ago.

"Christo's not at all like George," Natalie protested. George was a physicist, for heaven's sake.

"He broke my heart, " Sophy said flatly. "Just don't let Christo break yours."

* * *

He was on her doorstep shortly before seven.

Natalie had glimpsed Christo as he crossed the garden to come up the stairs, and she felt an immediate impulse to fly to the door. Not a good idea, she told herself.

The momentary panic she'd felt at awakening and discovering he was gone had evaporated during the day. She'd slept in.

Be honest, but not insane, she counseled herself. And so she waited until he knocked. Then she ran her hands down the sides of the casual yellow canvas pants she wore, and far more calmly and sedately than she felt, opened the door.

"Hey." He smiled at her. "Are we okay?"

She blinked at the seriousness in his eyes, despite the smile on his lips. "Okay?"

He lifted one broad shoulder, and his mouth twisted a little wryly. "I thought you might regret it."

Natalie swallowed. "Regret? Should I?"

"You know what I said about commitment, promises, the way I feel about long-term commitment…" Christo's voice trailed off and he looked at her expectantly.

"I know what you said," she agreed, keeping her voice even, betraying as little emotion as she could.

She didn't quite feel the equanimity she hoped she was expressing. But Christo wasn't telling her anything she hadn't heard from him already. He'd made no promises—except perhaps for promising that he would make none.

She'd assured him that she could handle it.

Now she reminded herself firmly that she could handle it. "I'm okay," she said and smiled at him, giving him her heart in her eyes whether he chose to see it or not.

What he saw she wasn't sure, but when she opened the door wider and waved him in, he entered, only pausing to give her a long and amazing kiss that had her bones melting before he moved on to the living room.

"Gotta finish these," he said, nodding at the bookcases they'd abandoned half in and half out of their spots on either side of the fireplace. "Then I thought we could grab a bite to eat. Yes?" He slanted a glance her way and the seriousness in his gaze had faded now. Only the smile remained.

"Yes," Natalie agreed. "Sounds good."

She helped him finish shifting the bookcases, and today as they bumped and touched, they laughed and gave in. They paused to touch, to kiss, to stroke, to stoke the fire building between them.

By the time Christo had the bookcase backs screwed into the wall studs and the shelves in place so that Laura's birthday bookshelves were a reality, the meal they were ready for had nothing to do with food.

"We can eat later, can't we?" Christo murmured, and Natalie nodded, taking his hand and starting toward the bedroom.

But, still holding her hand, he drew back, looking at her from beneath hooded lids. His skin over his cheekbones was taut and his face flushed. "Come to my place," he said. "Bigger bed. More room."

And one more demon to vanquish, Natalie thought, memories of that earlier disastrous night flitting across her mind. But she nodded resolutely. "Yes," she said.

The bedroom was much the same. The time of day—early evening—was the same. The setting sun spilled its light through wide slanted wooden blinds across the room, and the sun and shadow gave Christo tiger's stripes as he pulled his shirt over his head and then drew her into his arms.

Now she had new memories in the making, erasing the

old as Christo touched her gently, almost reverently, kissing her shoulders, her neck, then, stripping her shirt off her and removing her bra, he kissed his way down across her breasts and abdomen, kneeling before her, heading south.

Natalie's knees shook. Her fingers gripped his shoulders, then clenched in his hair as he skimmed off the rest of the clothes she wore and bore her back onto the bed. He shed his jeans and boxers, then nudged her knees apart and settled between them.

She reached for him, stroked him, made him catch his breath. His jaw tightened. A muscle ticked in his temple. A fine tremor seemed to course through him as he slid in. Easily. Perfectly. As if he were coming home.

This was the way she had dreamed it. The way she'd imagined it those three long years ago—she and Christo lovingly entwined, their bodies moving in unison as they gave each other the passion and love they shared.

After, he rolled off to lie on his back beside her, one arm over his head, the other outflung. His eyes were shut and she got another look at those glorious long lashes. She memorized them as well as the faint hint of evening stubble shadowing his cheeks and jaw.

She watched the rapid rise and fall of his chest, thought she could even see the way his heart hammered so strongly that the beats were visible against the wall of his chest.

Instinctively she reached out to lay a hand over it, to stroke his chest.

His eyes flicked open. His hand came up to wrap around hers, to hold it, still it, as he turned his head to meet her gaze.

"We need to talk."

"I thought we needed to eat," she said, smiling at him,

trying to deflect the seriousness she saw in his eyes. "I'm starved."

"In a minute. Or two." He gave her hand a squeeze, held it a moment, then let go, his eyes never leaving hers. "I have something I need to say."

"Something I don't want to hear?" Natalie guessed. It didn't take a mind reader to figure that out.

"No. Well, maybe. That's up to you." He gave his head a little shake. "What I need to say is, I know you still believe in marriage, that some day, fool that you are, you'll probably even want one." He looked at her for agreement.

Natalie gave an infinitesimal nod, waited, didn't say a word.

"And that's your choice," he went on. "Not mine. But yours. You want to get involved that way, go ahead."

"What?" She stared at him, certain she'd heard all the words, but still not sure what he'd said.

"If you meet a guy you want to marry, go for it," he said gruffly.

She blinked. "While I'm sleeping with you?"

His mouth twisted. "I expect you'd stop sleeping with me."

"I certainly would," Natalie said, annoyed.

"Don't get ticked," Christo said, rolling over onto his side, shoving up on one elbow and propping his head on his hand. "I'm just saying you should go for it. Don't let me—this—" he gave a wave toward their naked bodies "—get in your way."

"Of course not," Natalie said, wondering if wringing his neck would be too good for him.

He didn't detect the sarcasm in her voice. Just as well, probably.

"Well, good," he said, looking relieved. "I wouldn't want you to feel obligated. Just because I don't do entanglements and involvements, doesn't mean you shouldn't—if the opportunity arises."

He sounded as if he were giving a summation in a courtroom. Yes, wringing his neck was too good for him. "Well," Natalie said wryly, staring up at the ceiling, "that's good to know."

Christo sat up, looking cheerful, bright-eyed and eager. "Glad we've got it out in the open. I'm starving, too. Let's go eat."

She'd made a pact with the devil.

At least that's what it felt like.

But how could she change the rules now when she'd agreed to them at the outset? They weren't really rules, she supposed, but they were certainly expectations—or, in Christo's case, a complete lack thereof.

He was just making things clear.

He wouldn't have made love with her in the first place if she hadn't insisted that she didn't need protecting from her feelings for him. So she shouldn't be surprised to discover that he believed she was no more committed than he was.

She supposed she should consider him generous for telling her she could walk whenever she felt like it, no hard feelings.

Maybe someday she would.

Right now she was in a quandary. A part of her wanted to insist she cared as much as she ever had, that she loved him now with a far more honest and adult love than the infatuation she'd felt three years ago.

And another part didn't see any point in rocking the boat. She'd made her bed. Now she would lie in it. With him.

And if he didn't love her now or ever come to love her, she would have loved him—as her mother had loved her father—and she would learn to deal with it.

She offered to cook something for dinner, but he said there was a little place in Hermosa that had great seafood. They should go there.

A date? She almost asked. But she didn't. She didn't want to push her luck. She nodded. "Sounds good."

They took his Jaguar to the restaurant in Hermosa Beach. The food was great, Christo's company was every bit as enjoyable as she'd ever imagined it would be. They talked about everything from the law to fishing to the Dodgers' chances to win the pennant to when her mother was coming back.

"Another week, I think," Natalie said. "Can you manage?"

"Oh, yeah. Lisa's competent. Not as good as your mother—or you, for that matter," he said, his eyes warm as they met hers over the candle on the small restaurant table, "but I'm not having you back."

"Don't want me in your office?" Natalie teased.

His smile broadened. "Rather have you in my bed."

She was in his bed again, scant hours later. She went home to feed Herbie when they got back, but then Christo said, "Come to me."

And she did.

They made love once, twice. And once more before morning. Natalie stayed the night because she wanted to, and because Christo never indicated she should go.

When she opened her eyes in the morning, it was to find him already up and out of the shower. He was buttoning a long-sleeved dress shirt as he stood at the foot of the bed, but his eyes were not on the buttons. They were on her.

"Good morning." She smiled sleepily up at him and was gratified to see him smile in return.

"Morning. You going in to your office this morning?"

"Yes. But first I have to stop by Scott's and see how the new 'wife' is working out."

He nodded. "I was thinking I might try to get home a little early. Maybe we could go down to Redondo to the pier, catch a bite there, then go to a movie."

"I—" Natalie's reply caught in her throat "—can't."

Christo's fingers stilled on his shirt. "Can't?"

"My niece is spending the weekend with me. She's coming this evening."

"For the whole weekend?"

Natalie gave him a helpless shrug. "I didn't realize when I said I'd take her that I'd have a better offer. I think we'll go to the beach. You could join us."

But Christo shook his head. "No." He shoved his shirt into his trousers, then fastened his belt and looped a tie around his neck.

Putting on his armor, Natalie thought.

"I've got plenty to do," he said, his tone dismissive now. "But—"

He knotted the tie, then turned to face her. "Don't worry about it. Enjoy yourself. How about Sunday night?"

"For us, you mean?"

He nodded.

"Yes. I'll be having dinner with them when they come to pick her up. But after—unless you want to come along."

Once more he shook his head. "Have fun. Gotta go."

And just like that, he was gone.

* * *

Friday night with Jamii meant non-stop chatter and home-made tacos, baking cookies and watching DVDs.

Jamii wanted to invite Christo.

Natalie blanched, imagining what he would say to that. "You don't even know him!"

"Of course I know him," Jamii said huffily. "He's my friend. Me an' him an' Grandma go bowling together."

"Bowling?" Natalie simply stared at her niece.

"Uh-huh. So I do know him. Sometimes I eat breakfast with him when Grandma fixes it. An' he has good cereal. Cap'n Crackle."

Natalie hadn't noticed that when she'd been in his kitchen yesterday. But she began to realize that Jamii really did know him. Still he hadn't accepted her invitation this morning.

Which meant what? It wasn't too hard to figure out when she let herself think it through. Christo was fine relating to Jamii when she was with Laura. He liked Jamii and the relationship then, but not when it involved Natalie. Natalie, as the woman he took to bed, belonged in a different box in his life.

So she didn't expect to see him until Sunday night.

She and Jamii went to the beach Saturday afternoon. They spread their towels out at the top of the rise of the sand where it was still damp from the highest tides, but where at this time of day the water never reached. Unlike the old Jamii who used to make a beeline for the water, this one lay face down on the sand and began to dig a tunnel and make a castle. Natalie left her to it, picking up a book and trying to read.

The stream of chatter didn't let her get much read. But she kept her eyes on the pages, so she was unprepared for Jamii's sudden yelp. "Christo!"

"Hey, Jamii. What's up?"

Natalie's gaze jerked up to see the man himself standing there with his surfboard under his arm, dripping his way up from the water.

"Wanna build a castle with me? I'm making a whole city with lotsa tunnels, but I need a longer arm." She looked from his face to his arm hopefully.

"Jamii—" Natalie began to warn her off, not wanting her niece disappointed.

But to her surprise, Christo, after only a brief moment's hesitation, stuck his board in the sand and dropped down beside her.

"I could do that." He glanced at Natalie, but she couldn't read anything in his expression besides simple friendliness. "Hey."

"Er, hey." What else, after all, was there to say?

It was the most bizarre afternoon Natalie could ever remember.

On the surface it looked perfectly straightforward and normal. Anyone seeing them would just think that they were a family—two parents and a child, enjoying a Saturday afternoon on the beach together.

Of course, they were anything but.

In fact, she kept expecting Christo to finish whatever bit he was doing, then get up and leave. He didn't do "entanglements," after all.

But he stayed on. He was totally engaged in working with Jamii, talking to her, listening to her, patiently showing her how to create stability in the walls they were making.

"You could help," he said to Natalie once.

So she did. Some other children came by and wanted to help, too. Christo welcomed them all. He was like the Pied Piper to all of them. Jamii wasn't the only one who would have followed him anywhere by the time they had finished.

Even Natalie went down to the water with him to wash off the sand, then came back and dropped down on the towel. "Don't you want to rinse off?" she asked her niece.

Jamii just shook her head no.

"Suit yourself," Natalie said, resigned to getting Jamii to take a shower when they got back to the apartment. She tried to focus once more on her book when a shadow fell across her lap.

Christo, still sand-covered, had come back and stood frowning down at them. He flicked Natalie a puzzled look, then turned his attention to Jamii.

"What's up?"

"Nothin'." She didn't look at him, then, just started to dig again.

Once more Natalie thought he'd leave. Instead he dropped down to sit beside the little girl. "Why aren't you coming?"

Jamii shrugged. "Don't want to." She turned her face away.

Christo frowned, then looked to Natalie for the answer. "What's going on?" he asked her.

Natalie hesitated, then decided that Jamii's fear wasn't likely to go away until someone actually acknowledged it. So she told him what Dan had told her last night.

"Jamii went out in a boat with some friends. No one checked that her life preserver was on right. They hit some rough water and she tumbled out of the boat. The preserver came off and she nearly drowned."

"I did not!" Jamii protested, mortified.

But Christo's jaw tightened. "You could have," he said fiercely. But then the look on his face gentled. "That's rough."

"I like it okay," Jamii protested stubbornly. "I just don't wanta go in right now."

"I don't blame you."

He sat for a few more minutes in silence, his knees pulled up, his arms wrapped around them, as he sat and stared out at the water. The silence in him, the containment that accepted and absorbed the feelings of the other person reminded Natalie of how he'd been with the children in his office.

He'd had infinite patience with them. Now he showed the same patience to Jamii.

Natalie watched him warily, wondering what he would do.

He didn't talk now. Not for a long time. He never looked at Jamii either. Or at her, for that matter. Then, quietly, he began to speak.

"When I was your age," he said quietly, "I spent summers in Brazil at my grandmother's. It was winter there, but it was still warm, and some of my friends and I built a tree house. It was way up high and it swayed in the wind, and we thought it was the coolest place in the world. We rigged a pulley between two trees and did the Tarzan thing swooping between them." His mouth tipped at the corner and, from his expression, Natalie could see that he was remembering the time with fondness.

She thought Jamii, her attention caught now, her gaze fastened on him, could see that, too.

"It was great. I loved it," Christo went on. "But once when I was climbing up with some supplies, my hand slipped."

Jamii sucked in a sharp breath. "What happened?"

"I fell."

"A long way?"

He nodded. "Pretty far."

"Were you…okay?"

"I broke my arm," Christo said matter-of-factly. "Cracked a couple of ribs." He shrugged lightly. "Nothing too terrible. They all healed in a couple of months. But I couldn't go up in the tree again while I was healing. And then, when I had healed, I wouldn't go." He picked up a handful of sand and let it drizzle slowly out through his fingers. "I thought I'd fall."

"But if you hung on—" Jamii protested.

"I know. But I didn't think about that. I just kept remembering the falling. And I wouldn't go up again, even though my friends did and I could see all the fun they were still having. They tried to get me to come up, but I said I wasn't interested anymore."

Jamii's gaze narrowed, but she didn't say anything.

"I wasn't about to tell them I was scared." His voice was low enough that Natalie had to strain to hear. She shouldn't be eavesdropping, but she couldn't help it. Her fingers tightened on her book and she kept her gaze on the words, but she wasn't seeing them. She was totally focused on Christo.

So was Jamii, raptly. She chewed her lip. "And you never went up there again?"

"I wouldn't have," he admitted. "But one day when my friends weren't there my grandmother said, 'I'd like to see that tree house of yours.' I told her no. I said, 'It's not that great.' I said, 'It's too high up for you to get to.' And she said, 'It's pretty high, but I want to see it. I think I can do it if you'll go with me.'"

Jamii's mouth was open. She stared at him. "Did you?"

"No. But then she went over to it and started up the ladder by herself. So—" he took a breath "—I went after her. I had to make sure she didn't get hurt." His mouth twisted in a small self-deprecating grin. "And I discovered I could do it again after all."

"Which is what she wanted you to discover," Jamii, no fool, finished for him.

Christo nodded. He sat back on the sand, bracing his body with his hands. "Yep. And she was right. I could. Just like you can go in the water again." He looked at her now. "You know that, right?"

In the silence between them, Natalie heard a wave break, then another. Slowly, lips pursed, Jamii nodded. She hunched over her own upraised knees and wrapped her arms around them, too.

"Just like I knew it," Christo agreed. "But sometimes it helps to have someone to go with who understands."

"Like your grandma," Jamii said in a small voice.

"Uh-huh. So—" he slanted her a glance "—if you wanted to try sticking a toe or two in, I'd go with you."

Natalie held her breath.

Jamii squeezed her arms around her legs. She chewed her lip. She didn't speak.

Neither did Christo. He just sat there, staring out at the horizon, completely unhurried, as if he had nothing better to do than wait for an eight-year-old girl to make up her mind.

"Could I ride on your shoulders?" Jamii asked him at last.

Christo flicked her a quick glance. "Down to the water? Sure, if you want."

"And you wouldn't drop me?"

"Never."

"We wouldn't go out far, right?"

"Just as far as you want."

"And you'll bring me back when I want?"

"I will."

"Even if I change my mind?"

"Even if you change your mind." He didn't move. Only waited.

So did Jamii. Then, slowly she unfolded herself and stood up, then squared her small shoulders. She looked at the ocean, then back at Christo and gave one quick nod of her head. "Okay," she said. "Let's go."

He stood up and held out a hand to Jamii, then swung her onto his shoulders. Then he looked back over his shoulder at Natalie and held out a hand to her as well.

She thought the hand was just to pull her to her feet. But when she was upright, he didn't let go.

He didn't do anything else. Didn't brush his hand across her arm. Didn't come close enough to touch her cheek with his lips. It was very circumspect.

And intimate. Because it was not simply sex. It was a connection outside of bed. The two of them together were a couple, walking hand in hand down the beach toward the pier.

While they walked through shin-high waves that broke and foamed around their ankles, he talked more to her than to Jamii. In fact, Jamii might as well not have been there at all.

The conversation was casual—about the weather, about the water. About ideas for more woodworking projects he had. It was for Jamii—Natalie knew that. And yet, as their fingers were laced and his thumb rubbed against the side of her hand, and neither of them glanced up at Jamii on his shoulders, Natalie couldn't help believing it was about something else.

A wave surged against their knees, rocking them a little, and Natalie heard Jamii suck in a sharp breath. Christo kept right on talking without missing a beat. His fingers tightened on hers, but he never faltered, never misstepped.

Only when they reached the pier and turned to walk back the way they'd come did he actually address a comment to Jamii.

"Want to go back to your towel now or do you want to get your feet wet?"

There was a long pause—long enough for Natalie to imagine Jamii was going to opt for going back to the towel. She might have done so, at Jamii's age.

But Jamii, bless her heart, was made of sterner stuff. And had Christo in her corner. "I guess I could stick my toes in."

Christo smiled. He turned his head to look up at her. "Do you want me to put you down here or do you want to walk in?"

"Here. With you."

He let go of Natalie's hand to reach up and lift the little girl off his shoulders, but he didn't set her on the ground. Instead he walked back to where the water was just beginning to lap against the shore, and he sat down on the sand, with Jamii on his lap. Natalie sat down beside them.

Foamy water from broken waves rushed up alongside and lapped at their legs. Natalie expected Jamii to go rigid. And she saw the instant of fear in Jamii's eyes, the sudden tension.

But Christo had her securely wrapped in his arms, and he didn't let go until the water had receded again. Then he scooped up a handful of wet sand and drizzled it on Jamii's legs.

She laughed. Then, to Natalie's surprise, Jamii wriggled off Christo's lap onto the wet sand so she could do the same to him. Another wave broke while she was scooping up the wet sand, and she tensed momentarily, then continued.

Natalie's gaze met Christo's over Jamii's head. He smiled. So did she. It was a moment of perfect communion.

He stood up then and held out a hand to Jamii. "Come with me?" It was an offer. An invitation.

Jamii, after only the briefest of hesitations, put her hand in his. Then, standing together, they faced the waves.

Jamii was not an easy sell when it came to feeling comfortable in the water again. But for the rest of the afternoon Christo persevered. He acted as if he hadn't said he wouldn't spend the day with them. He acted like he was perfectly happy to be there.

When at last they called it a day and walked back across the sand to the apartment, he walked with them.

"Say thank you for everything," Natalie prompted Jamii when they reached the garden. "Christo did you a great favor today."

Jamii nodded. "Thank you," she said to him, and Natalie could hear the sincerity in her voice.

"You're welcome," Christo said gravely. "But you know you could have done it on your own."

Jamii bobbed her head. "But it helps to have someone there for you, like you said. Will you come down with me tomorrow?"

"Jamii!" Natalie protested.

But Christo nodded. "Sure."

"And will you have pizza with us tonight?"

Natalie's face went scarlet, imagining that Christo would think she'd given Jamii the idea to try to create entanglements where he didn't want them. "I'm sorry," she said. "Jamii, you mustn't presume—"

"He has pizza with Grandma and me sometimes. Don't you, Christo?" her niece demanded.

"Sometimes I do," Christo agreed. He lifted his gaze and met Natalie's almost defiantly. "Laura considers it her duty to feed me when I seem at loose ends." There was a hint of something in his face that she couldn't read.

"Are you at loose ends tonight?" she asked warily.

"I am."

"Then I guess you'd better have pizza with us."

"I guess I should."

It was like having one of her long-ago fantasies come to life—opening the door of the apartment and having Christo leaning against the doorjamb smiling at her, then holding out a bottle of wine.

She took it wordlessly, the mere sight of him robbing her of words. He was freshly shaved, the stubbled jaw of this afternoon smooth now. His hair was damp but freshly washed and combed. He wore a clean pair of faded jeans and an equally faded red T-shirt. Nothing special.

But in Christo's case, it definitely wasn't the clothes that made the man.

And all the desire she'd assured herself she intended to keep well tamped down and controlled seemed to rise right up and smack her. She stared wordlessly at him.

And, heaven help her, Christo stared back.

It was the way he looked when he made love to her. His eyes darkened. His smile faded. He took a step toward her—and Jamii appeared.

"Hi, Christo! Come see the book I'm writing?"

Christo blinked, then dragged his gaze away from Natalie and focused on her niece. "Sure."

While Natalie tore up greens for a salad, she listened to Christo and Jamii talking in the living room. He paid just as much attention to Jamii's literary efforts as he had to making her comfortable in the water. He listened intently as Jamii told him all about the care and feeding of hamsters and guinea pigs.

Natalie marveled at his focus. But then, when she called them to come and eat, she felt that his focus had shifted to her. Or maybe it hadn't—it was just her oversensitized nerve endings and imagination.

Whatever it was, every time Natalie looked up, it seemed that Christo did, too. Their gazes would connect and sizzle, then slide slowly away. When he passed her a glass of wine, their fingers brushed and it felt as erotic as when he'd learned the contours of her naked body. And from the speculative look he gave her, she dared to imagine he felt the same way.

Watching him eat the pizza was worse. It had the effect of making her remember vividly the scene of the young gorgeous Albert Finney in the old film *Tom Jones,* eating the chicken and licking his fingers, and causing every woman who watched it to experience a serious spike in her heart rate.

Not that Christo was licking his fingers. He was perfectly well-mannered. It was her fevered brain that was working overtime.

In desperation, she shoved back her chair and stood up. "I'll just go make some coffee."

But the moment she was in the kitchen fumbling with the coffeemaker, he was there behind her and she spun around, nearly knocking the dirty dinner plates he carried out of his hands.

"What are you doing?" she demanded sharply.

He raised a single brow. "Setting a good example?"

He put his plate and hers into the sink, and immediately behind him, Jamii appeared carrying her own, which she deposited there also.

"Oh." Natalie felt idiotic. And ridiculously aware. "Thank you."

"My pleasure. Do you want me to do that?" He was looking at the coffeemaker, with which she didn't seem to be making any progress. "Let me," he said, and took the basket out of her hands. He filled the reservoir with water, then opened the cupboard and got out a filter, which he fitted into the basket.

She opened the cupboard to get a grip on her sanity and, incidentally, to find the coffee. It wasn't there.

Christo just went to the refrigerator—since when had her mother kept the coffee in the refrigerator?—and took out a bag. He measured some beans into the electric coffee grinder she didn't even know her mother had, then pressed it with the heel of his hand until the redolence of fresh-ground coffee filled the air.

Dumping the coffee into the basket, he put it back into the coffeemaker, then flicked on the switch and leaned back against the cabinet, folding his arms across his chest. He smiled at her.

"I don't…make coffee here often," she mumbled.

"I do," he said. Then he leaned forward and, very gently, kissed her on the lips.

He was melting her right where she stood. She couldn't move. Stood mesmerized by his kiss. Wanted it to go on and on and on. Wanted him to wrap his arms around her as he'd done before. Wanted to wrap hers around him.

She leaned into him.

"Wanta watch a movie, Christo?" Jamii's voice floated in from the living room causing them both to jump back.

Christo cleared his throat. Adjusted his jeans.

"We've got *The Bad News Bears* and *Cinderella*," Jamii called.

"Cinderella?" Natalie arched a brow at him. She still trembled. Still felt the shivers of unrequited desire running up and down her arms and legs.

Christo gave her a wry smile. "I'm hoping for the other one."

"You don't have to stay."

"I'm staying."

Their gazes met, locked.

"It's ready," Jamii called.

"Go on," Natalie said. "I'll bring the coffee."

One more kiss that left her weak-kneed and then he joined Jamii in the living room. Natalie stood gripping the kitchen countertop, taking deep breaths and praying for a little sanity. When the coffee was ready, she poured them each a mug full and carried it into the living room.

"Sit here," Jamii wriggled over next to Christo and left Natalie the spot on the end.

She sat down, and with Jamii between them, they watched the movie. Or Jamii watched the movie—not *Cinderella,* thank God.

Natalie watched Christo's hands as they cradled his coffee mug. She watched him stretch out his legs and could not tear her gaze from the flex of easy muscles beneath the soft denim of his jeans, unless it was to contemplate his bare feet.

She was aware of the couch shifting every time he moved. She knew when he stretched one arm along the back of the sofa. Close. But not close enough to touch. Did he know how close?

The movie was funny. Jamii was in stitches, giggling madly. Christo laughed, too. Then he shifted again and his fingers brushed against her neck. They played with her hair, they made the nape of her neck tingle and sent involuntary shivers down the length of her spine. She was so exquisitely aware of him that she couldn't think of anything else at all.

She turned her head to look at him. And he looked back. Their eyes met. His fingers brushed lightly along the back of her neck. She trembled. He smiled.

Exactly when Natalie realized that Jamii wasn't laughing now but was asleep between them, she didn't know. But Christo obviously knew. He moved carefully, easing himself up and scooping the sleeping child into his arms. "Where do you want her?"

And Natalie tore her gaze away from his to clamber to her feet and lead the way into her mother's bedroom. She pulled back the covers on the bed and Christo bent to lay Jamii down. He brushed the little girl's hair away from her face, then stepped back.

Christo was so close to her—and she was so aware of him—that she could hear the soft intake of his breath. And her own caught in her throat as he turned to face her, touched her arm and began to guide her backwards out of the room.

It was as if they were dancing, his hooded gaze hot and hungry as it met hers. His fingers slid up her arm and over her shoulder to the nape of her neck, echoing his earlier touches, heightening her awareness.

They were in the hallway now, and her back was against the wall, and he bent his head, his lips coming down inexorably to meld with hers.

They parted under his touch, opened to him as they had last time, as she longed to do. She slid her arms around him, drawing him closer, pressing against him, reveling in the hard strength of his body against the soft curves of hers. He slid his hands under her shirt, caressed her back, cupped her breasts.

"Aunt Nat!"

Christo jerked back, chest heaving. Natalie straightened sharply, and looked around, relieved not to see her niece standing there staring at them.

"What?" She tugged her shirt down, then slipped past Christo to go to Jamii. "What's wrong?"

"I fell asleep! We didn't get to see the end of the movie!" Jamii sat up in the bed, staring up at her, crushed. "Can I see it now?"

"Not…now," Natalie said, wishing her heart would stop hammering so frantically. "Tomorrow. In the morning."

Jamii sighed and slumped against the pillows. "Is Christo still here?"

Before Natalie could answer, Christo said from the doorway, "On my way home." He sounded calm and steady, and Natalie wondered how he managed it.

"Will we go swimming tomorrow again?" Jamii asked him.

"I'll come and get you in the morning. Go to sleep now."

"But—"

"You heard him. Sleep," Natalie commanded. "Or you won't go."

Jamii made a face, but she lay back down. Natalie bent and kissed her good-night, then turned and followed Christo back into the living room.

The needs were still there, thrumming inside her, even as she spoke. "We can't—" she said almost apologetically.

"I know."

He sounded terse. Tense. Dissatisfied. All of the above.

He gave her a hard, fierce, almost angry kiss and stalked quickly out the door.

CHAPTER FIVE

IT HAD been a damn fool idea—spending the day with Natalie and Jamii.

He never should have done it, Christo thought. He lay in his bed and tried not to remember spending the night there with Natalie. But like everything else with Natalie, it didn't work.

Like today. He'd turned down her suggestion to go to the beach with them. He hadn't spelled it out. He didn't need to. He'd been honest with her. He'd told her he didn't do forever, didn't want complications, commitments, all that sort of thing.

It simply made sense not to create entanglements by going to the beach with her and her niece.

And then he'd done it anyway.

Well, not intentionally. At least he hadn't been stupid enough to do that. But when he'd spotted them on the sand as he'd come out of the water after going surfing, he'd simply found his feet heading in their direction.

He knew Jamii, of course. She stayed with her grandmother often, and he liked her. She was far less complicated than most of the kids he dealt with on a regular basis.

He liked her fresh, open acceptance of life. She was like a small version of Laura.

And she didn't half remind him of Natalie as well.

But he hadn't gone to say hi only to Jamii. He'd missed spending Friday night with Natalie in his bed. Two nights he'd spent with her now, and somehow last night, without her, he'd felt far more alone than he usually did.

Maybe it was because he had worked late, then come home to see the light on in Laura's apartment, to know they were up there—he could even hear Jamii's giggle—and he'd wanted to go up as well.

He hadn't, of course. No way. No point. Bad idea.

Instead he'd worked on one of his arguments for a case he was in conference about next week. But out of his window he'd kept noticing the light in Laura's apartment.

And then he'd noticed when it went off.

She'd gone to bed. And dear God, he wanted to be there with her. He wanted to spend the night making love to her, then holding her, watching her fall asleep in his arms.

She had once.

No one ever had before. He couldn't remember a single woman he'd slept with who had settled against him that way, who'd snuggled close and shut her eyes and simply trusted him like that.

Natalie had because Natalie was not like the women he had affairs with, or noninvolved relationships with. Or whatever you called these liaisons that had everything to do with physical needs and nothing to do with the heart.

Natalie, like her mother, had everything to do with the heart.

He shouldn't have slept with her. And at the same time he said that, he knew he could hardly wait to do it again.

Was that why he'd sought them out today? Was that why he'd stayed?

He twisted in his bed, sprawled and shifted and punched his pillow and tried to answer that.

But he couldn't come up with a good answer. Not one that his lawyer's mind would admit or accept. He always enjoyed seeing Jamii. But it was less Jamii's company than Natalie's that he'd been angling for. Just having her there, watching and listening while he and Jamii were talking had felt—he punched the pillow again—right, somehow.

And, of course, he was glad he'd stayed when he discovered Jamii's fear of the water. He knew paralyzing fear. He'd had it himself. What his grandmother had done for him was something he'd always been grateful for. It seemed a small enough thing to share it with Natalie's niece.

And whether Natalie knew it or not, Christo knew that her niece had overcome her fear only in part because of his confidence in her. It was also having Natalie there. Natalie was the one Jamii knew, the one she loved and trusted. He told Jamii the story. He helped her. But he could not have done it alone.

She needed the love and acceptance of her family as well.

He wasn't sure Natalie understood that. But maybe she did. She was Laura's daughter.

Dear God. He couldn't believe he was sleeping with Laura's daughter.

He was going to have to stop. Soon.

But not yet.

Natalie opened the door almost before he knocked the next morning. "I have a tremendous favor to ask."

"Oh? That sounds promising." Christo grinned. "Wash your back? Make slow, sweet love to you?"

"I wish," Natalie said frankly. "I wonder if you would watch Jamii."

He blinked. "I said I'd take her swimming."

"Yes, but I figured I'd go, too," Natalie said. "So you wouldn't be watching her precisely. I would be. But I—we—the business—has a job I need to do."

Christo's eyes narrowed. "You need to be somebody's wife?"

Natalie nodded. "Somebody's hostess in this case. One of our best clients is having a group of business colleagues out on his yacht. He was expecting Rosalie to do the honors. But Rosalie, I'm sorry to say, got food poisoning last night. Sophy just called me this morning."

"And Sophy can't do it because—"

"Because she gets seasick. I'm it, I'm afraid. I can see if Harry's mother would mind having Jamii for the day. Jamii likes Harry and vice-versa, but—"

"No," Christo said, surprising himself. "I'll take her."

"You're a saint," Natalie said and threw her arms around him. She kissed him, stunned him, really, that a swift simple kiss could have that much power.

She shouldn't have asked him. She didn't know what else to do.

And he could have said no.

She was surprised he hadn't.

Natalie took her cell phone with her. "Call me," she said, "if you have any problems. Dan and Kelly should be back by suppertime. They know you're taking over for me. I rang them this morning. They say they'll take you to dinner instead of me. It was part of the deal," she explained.

"They don't need to feed me dinner," Christo said promptly.

But he'd said no to coming out with her and Jamii on Saturday, too, and look what had happened that day.

"Whatever you want," she told him.

"You," he said.

Natalie was holding on to that thought.

She'd been afraid, after last night's unconsummated ending, that he might want to be finished with her already. She would not have been surprised if he'd called today and said he couldn't make it.

But he'd come. He'd even flirted a little. So their affair had lived another day. She wondered if she should notch them on a bedpost. Though even as she thought it, she knew she shouldn't be facetious. She was riding high now. But she was riding for a fall, and she knew it.

"Believe," her mother always told her. "Trust. Hope."

"And you'll get kicked in the teeth," her more realistic daughter had countered after her father's defection.

"You don't believe that," Laura had chided her.

And Natalie knew she didn't. So she'd just keep believing, trusting and hoping that maybe someday Christo would realize he loved her, too.

It might not have been his ideal day, but spending it with Jamii Ross taught Christo a lot more about her aunt Natalie.

He learned she could play the piano, but she never liked to practice. He learned she liked spinach and artichokes but hated kale and brussels sprouts. He learned she had always wanted to travel, to see different places, but she hadn't got to go yet.

"Except to Mexico," Jamii said. "She went with us last year to Cabo."

He learned she had been the co-leader of Jamii's Brownie troop last year and would have done it again this year, but she had to work too many hours with her new job and she was really, really busy.

"Too busy to even have a boyfriend," Jamii reported, as she concentrated on building a turret for their sand castle.

"Was she?" Christo didn't examine too closely why he was glad to hear it.

"Do you have a girlfriend?" Jamii asked him.

"I—"

"'Cause if you don't, maybe you could have Aunt Nat."

"Tempting," Christo said.

He didn't let himself think just how much.

Natalie had barely come in and kicked off her shoes and sank down on the sofa when her phone rang.

"Hey."

She smiled, warmed at the sound of his voice. "How'd it go?" she asked. "She's gone, I see."

"She's gone," he agreed. "We had a good time. I know all your secrets now."

"Oh, dear," Natalie laughed. "Even about Billy Hardesty?"

"Who's Billy Hardesty?"

"Good. I've got one secret left." She tipped her head back on the sofa and shut her eyes, just enjoying the sound of his voice in her ear.

"Not for long," Christo promised silkily. "Are you hungry?"

"A little. There was plenty of food and no time to eat it. I was run off my feet."

"We can solve that," he said. There was a click.

She thought he'd hung up and she felt momentarily bereft. Then she heard footsteps and realized that the click had been the front door opening and he was standing over her, smiling down at her. He flicked the phone off.

"C'mon," he said. And he scooped her up and carried her out the door and down the stairs.

"What are you—? Where are you—?" But she didn't finish. She didn't have to. She knew.

He kicked open the door to his place and carried her straight down the hall to the living room where he set her gently on the sofa. Then he sank down beside her and drew her into his arms.

She went willingly, happily.

Was she supposed to resist? It wasn't possible. It was a dream come true.

Believe. Trust. Hope.

All the words her mother had given her—words she held close to her heart—even as she held Christo there.

Believe. Trust. Hope. *And love.*

She would give him everything she had and hope that it was enough. There was no choice.

She had to.

It felt as though he'd been waiting forever.

She'd only been out of his bed two nights. *Two!* Mere hours. And yet it felt like a lifetime. He'd heard her car, seen her come into the garden, and he'd gone after her almost as soon as she'd gone upstairs.

Now he massaged her aching feet and made her whimper with pleasure.

"Who's Billy Hardesty?" He grinned, running his fingers along the sole of her foot, making her squirm.

"Oooh, you're evil." She gasped and giggled, writhed and twisted. "I'll never tell."

He ran his hands up her legs. "Never?" His fingers found her, teased her. "Never say never."

Her eyes were bright and laughing as she tugged him down on top of her. "He's the first boy who ever kissed me. We were five."

"Ah. I guess I can let him live, then. As long as he doesn't make a habit of it."

"No one makes a habit of it," she told him.

And Christo found himself thinking, *I will.*

But he didn't let himself think of the ramifications of the thought. He only kissed her thoroughly and set about loving her. She returned the favor.

Christo wasn't used to giving up control, but how could he refuse her? Besides, she didn't ask. She simply touched. She, too, kissed, nibbled, caressed, laved.

She wrung him out. Left him spent and gasping. Left him sated and, at the same time, wanting more.

Wanting her. Because this—whatever it was—wasn't enough. Somewhere deep inside Christo felt an odd persistent sort of ache he'd never felt before.

Knew the temptation to say three words he'd never said. Words he swore he didn't believe in.

And realizing what those words were, Christo knew a fear as paralyzing as the one he'd helped Jamii vanquish.

He didn't love Natalie!

He couldn't.

CHAPTER SIX

WHEN Natalie looked back she couldn't put her finger on the moment she realized that something was wrong. There was no clear defining instant.

The truth was, there had probably always been something wrong. She'd just been too preoccupied with wishful thinking to admit it.

Or maybe with the misplaced confidence of the young and in love, she had believed she could change Christo's mind.

She'd been honest with him, after all. She had said yes, that three years ago if they had made love, she would have wanted the whole thing—love, marriage, happily ever after.

But not admitting in her heart that she still felt the same way, she hadn't been as honest with herself.

She'd assured herself that knowing what Christo wanted was enough, that she was a big girl now, that she could cope with the limitations he imposed on their relationship.

Well, not quite.

Their relationship—or whatever you called it—was fine as far as it went. Heavens, being loved—in a physical sense—by Christo was amazing.

But it didn't go to the heart.

Natalie, dreamer that apparently she still was, had dared

to hope it would. She couldn't imagine that she wouldn't be able to convince him that what she felt for him was strong enough, stable enough, mature enough to stand up to whatever disillusionment he'd endured in the past.

Which just went to show, she supposed, how immature her love really was.

Or maybe not. But it wasn't enough. She knew that. She loved him—and he was pulling back.

The desire was still there. He still said every morning, "Will I see you tonight?" He was still an eager, generous lover in bed. He could make her twist and writhe and shudder with her need of him.

But he didn't hold her in his arms.

Not anymore. When she woke in the night now, she was alone. He was in the bed, yes, but removed. Distant. Only if he fell asleep still holding her did they share that closeness. If he was awake, he had pulled away.

At first she thought it might having nothing to do with their relationship. It could be his work, she thought. He had a lot of difficult, painful cases.

"Is something wrong?" Natalie asked the first morning after she'd experienced the distance. They were sitting in the kitchen. She'd made breakfast for the two of them before she went back to her mother's to dress for work.

Christo, who had come in silently, poured a cup of coffee and was staring at the front page of the paper, didn't answer at first.

When she repeated the question, he looked startled, then edgy. He'd shaken his head. "No."

It was all the answer she got out loud. His silence said much more.

He started running in the mornings. She'd wake up and

find he had already left her. He never invited her to go with him. Never talked about why he was going now when he hadn't gone before.

And Natalie didn't ask because she sensed instinctively that there were questions now he wouldn't answer.

Was this the way it always happened? she wondered. Was this how he ended all his affairs? Or did she dare still hope?

"I've made a reservation for Friday." Laura's voice was so bright and cheerful in the face of her own grim mood that Natalie had to take a deep breath before answering.

"Everything well, then?" she asked. It would be some comfort to know that things were going well somewhere.

"We haven't killed each other," Laura said drily. "So all things considered, it's going fine." She sighed. "It's an adjustment," she said. "Gran wants to dance polkas. She has no patience. But she's making progress."

"Is she all right alone?"

"Yes. And I'll come back and stay with her for a while in a month or two. But right now I need to get back to my life and she needs to adjust here."

"Sounds good."

"It will be a good time," Laura said, "with Christo leaving, I'll have a chance to catch up on office paperwork without him underfoot."

"Leaving?" Natalie dropped the spoon in the pot of oatmeal she was stirring for their breakfast. "Christo?"

"He didn't tell you? Well, no, I suppose he wouldn't since you're not working with him now." Laura sounded completely unconcerned. She, of course, was also unaware that Natalie was at that moment in Christo's kitchen.

No, I'm not working with him. I'm sleeping with him,
Natalie thought with just a hint of hysteria. Why should he
tell her? She was the woman in his bed for the moment.
Nothing more. Nothing less.

"He's delivering a paper at a conference in Sacramento,"
Laura told her. "The conference runs over the weekend. So
it will be perfect. Provided I survive the next few days."
Laura laughed.

Natalie did, too, albeit a bit hollowly. "Shall I pick you
up at the airport then?"

"That would be fantastic." Her mother rattled off the
details of the flight and Natalie wrote them down with one
hand and kept stirring with the other. She had just hung up
the phone when Christo appeared in the doorway.

"Morning." He poured himself a cup of coffee and
flashed her a smile.

It was friendly but, looking closely, she could see that
there was nothing particularly personal about it. It was
almost as if he had built a wall between them.

There was certainly nothing to indicate they had just
spent hours in each other's arms, that they had touched and
tasted and known each other in the most intimate of ways.

"Good morning," she said evenly. "My mother just rang.
She's coming home on Friday."

He nodded, then paused reflectively, as if something had
occurred to him, but he didn't say anything, just sat down
in front the bowl of oatmeal she put at his place on the table
and began to eat.

"She and Grandma are ready to be done with each other
for the time being," she went on. "And she said it was a
good time to come because you'd be away." She looked at
him expectantly.

He nodded. Didn't say a word.

"In Sacramento delivering a paper," she said casually, pleased with how disinterested she sounded as she wiped down the countertop and turned to run water in the empty oatmeal pot.

It wasn't even as if she cared that he was going. It was that he hadn't thought enough of their relationship to bother telling her.

Christo nodded. "That's right." But he offered no further comment, no explanation, made no attempt to engage her interest.

Because he obviously didn't want her interest, Natalie thought.

She heard him set down the coffee mug and turned to see him steeple his fingers in front of his face. He stared at them wordlessly, as if she weren't even in the room.

Natalie turned back to the pot and began scrubbing it with a vengeance under the running water. "So I'll be going home then, too, obviously," she said, barely glancing over her shoulder, focusing instead on the pot.

There was a long silence. The only sound was the running water and the furious action of the scouring pad in Natalie's hand.

Then Christo said, "So it would probably be a good time for us to end things, too."

Natalie didn't even look around. She kept right on scrubbing the pot until it shone. Then she rinsed it and shut off the water before she finally turned around to face him as she picked up a dish towel and began to dry the pot.

Only then, when she could say it with equanimity and just the faintest tightness in her throat, did she speak. "If that's what you want."

For an instant he hesitated. Then he nodded almost curtly and stood up. "I think that would be best."

That afternoon there was no message on her voice mail saying, "I'll see you tonight." There was no brisk single knock on the door.

Natalie was home in Laura's apartment all evening. She read a book. She washed her hair. She watched TV. She didn't know if Christo was home or not.

She tried to pretend she didn't care.

She didn't see him. Not that she'd expected to. Not after this morning's flat dispassionate, *it would probably be a good time for us to end things, too.*

A part of her had spent the day hoping he'd realize that there was more than nights in bed between them, more than sex, more than whatever physical desire might roar through their veins.

But as she sat in the living room in silence, she knew it wasn't going to happen.

His lights were on across the garden. He was home. No doubt about that. Just as there was no doubt he was going to stay there by himself.

At first Natalie tried consoling herself with the knowledge that at least she hadn't humiliated herself this time. But the longer she sat there, the more she knew that wasn't enough.

They had played this game his way, by his rules. As far as he knew she'd obeyed them all. And, heaven help her, she would live by the consequences of her actions, however painful those consequences were.

But if she was going to have to live on this for the rest of her life she wanted more.

"More," she told Herbie firmly aloud, as much to hear herself say it as to convince the cat.

He was sprawled on the rocking chair sound asleep, anyway. He didn't move. Or care. Not even when she got up, brushed her teeth, combed her hair, put on a bit of lip gloss, went out and locked the door behind her.

She didn't let herself stop to think. She knew what would happen if she did.

Instead she walked briskly down the stairs and rapped sharply on Christo's back door. It took a minute, maybe longer, for the door to open and Christo to stand there, looking at her.

Something unreadable flickered in his gaze. Mostly he looked surprised and maybe a little confused. He straightened at the sight of her and raised his brows. "What's wrong?"

"Nothing's wrong," Natalie said. "I just got to thinking, if we're ending it, let's do it right. Let's know it's over."

"What?"

She held out a hand to him and gave him her brightest bravura smile and said recklessly, "I think we should have one for the road."

Was he supposed to say no?

Maybe he should have.

He'd spent far too much time thinking about Natalie over the past couple of weeks. She was always on his mind in ways no other woman ever had been. She got under his skin and he couldn't compartmentalize her the way he had with the others.

He wanted to be with her, talk to her, laugh with her, walk on the beach with her. He wanted to build sand castles with her, watch videos with her, do a hundred other things besides just make love to her.

It was getting to be an obsession, he told himself.

Last weekend, when he'd first felt a prickling fear of his lack of control of the situation, he'd decided that his trip to Sacramento would provide a natural breathing space. Even then, for a split second, he'd entertained the idea of asking her to come with him.

Only a split second, though.

Then sanity had prevailed.

But if she wanted a last time, by God he'd give it to her, he thought as he took her hand and drew her into his house, then shut the door behind her.

What difference did one more time make?

And she was right. It would be better if they both knew this was their last time. Closure. No surprises. No regrets.

He didn't speak as he led her down the hall. He only paused to drop the heavy legal book he'd been staring mindlessly at all evening in hopes that it would inspire him to great insights—or help him sleep once he went to bed.

Now he had something better. Natalie.

Suddenly he had to have her. He tugged her shirt over her head, ran suddenly unsteady hands down her sides, peeled off her shorts. She settled into the duvet on his bed and opened her arms to him.

And, heaven help him, Christo couldn't get out of his clothes fast enough. This time she didn't help him, but just lay there watching him, waiting for him to fumble out of his dress shirt, to rip off his tie. He hadn't changed when he'd come home. He'd just slumped in the chair with his book, determined to wait until it was time to go to bed.

"Bit slow tonight, aren't you?" she murmured, sending his temperature up another couple of degrees.

He nearly ripped the buttons off his shirt, then dropped his trousers and kicked off his shoes. He came down on the bed beside her then, reaching for her.

She shook her head and caught his hands. "No."

"No?" He couldn't believe his ears.

She laughed and reached down for his feet. "I'm not having my last memories of you naked in bed with your socks on."

Christo laughed, too, as she bent down and peeled them off, then ran her fingers over his feet and up his legs. But it was a strained laugh, and once his socks were disposed of, he bore her back on the bed, needing the feel of her body against his, hungry for the embrace of her arms.

His body wanted fulfillment now, this very minute. His will power, better disciplined, made him slow down. It made him take his time with her—savor every caress, every touch—get his fill.

At the same time he memorized the look on her face as his hands roved over her body, absorbed every detail—the curve of her ear, the tiny mole on her shoulder, the impossibly long lashes that fluttered as he kissed her eyelids. He drew in the lime-and-coconut scent of her shampoo as he nuzzled her hair and the faintly salty tang of her skin wherever his lips and tongue touched her. He stroked her and made her back arch, made her toes curl, made her reach for him.

But he resisted. "Wait," he told her. "Wait."

And when at least neither of them could stand waiting a second longer, he came over her and slid into her, relishing the slick tight warmth that enveloped him as her arms came around him and her fingers raked his back.

The moment was so perfect that Christo simply froze, desperate to capture it, to make it last.

Then Natalie moved. And the sensation of her body against his shattered the last remnants of his control.

He surged against her, meeting her as their bodies moved in perfect counterpoint, until he felt her body spasm around him.

One last time he lost himself in her. Then he no longer knew where he ended and she began.

Closure, Natalie thought for days afterward, was highly overrated.

Certainly she had her memories, and some of them made that last night in Christo's arms were absolutely amazing.

But they didn't change anything.

She had still left his bed before dawn, though he'd been awake this time. She'd moved to get out of bed and he'd caught her hand and said, "Stay."

For an instant, she'd dared hope he meant forever. But then he said, "It's only three. We've got time."

But Natalie knew that time had run out. "I need some sleep," she'd said, marveling at how matter-of-fact she sounded. "And you do, too, so you can get things all ship-shape before you leave."

It was the single time in the last couple of days that she'd mentioned anything to do with their lives beyond the bed. It was an acknowledgment of reality. Nothing more.

Christo hadn't argued. He'd seen the logic of it, the reason. Christo was all about logic and reason, after all. He'd let her go, had watched her dress. But before she left, he'd climbed out of bed and pulled on a pair of shorts.

"I'll see you home."

"I'll be fine," she said, not at all sure she could stand the civility of this last gesture.

But Christo insisted. "I'll see you to Laura's door."

They went in silence. He didn't touch her now. But she could feel his presence right behind her. Could hear him breathing. Their arms brushed as he opened the door for her and let her go past him.

Natalie held her head high. Refused to allow herself the tears she knew would have come by now if she'd walked home alone. She got to the top of Laura's stairs with her dignity intact, and put the key in the lock before Christo could do it for her. Then, with the door open, she turned and held out her hand, even managed a smile.

"Good night."

He didn't reply, just stood looking down at her in the darkness. Then he took her hand, held it, squeezed it for just a moment, then let it go. She heard him swallow.

"Sleep well," he said. Then abruptly he turned and was gone.

Natalie stood there in the stillness, waiting for the sound of his back door to open and close. It never did. She heard the gate instead.

She went inside quickly and went to the window in time to see him disappearing down the walk toward The Strand, then hopping over the wall to hit the sand and take off running.

She headed straight for the bedroom, for all the good it would do her.

"Sleep well," she echoed his words out loud as she lay down and stared at the ceiling.

Yeah, right.

* * *

"Are you all right, dear?" Laura stopped mid-sentence in her description of how well Grandma's recovery was going to study Natalie closely.

Natalie, who had invited her mother over for meat loaf because she truly did want to hear about her grandmother while at the same time she did not want to run into Christo, smiled brightly. "Of course. Why wouldn't I be?"

"You're very quiet."

"I'm generally quiet," Natalie reminded her. "Dan was the noisy one."

"Yes, but you've barely said two words since I got home last week. Every time I ask you how things went—even when you worked with Christo—you just say, fine." Laura was regarding her suspiciously over a glass of wine.

Natalie shrugged negligently. "Because they were fine. No problems at all. Why? Did he say there were?" She frowned now as she put a helping of green beans on her plate.

"No. He hasn't said anything, either. He works all the time. Never even stops by for dinner now. He stays at the office until nearly bedtime."

"Maybe he has a lot to catch up on."

Laura nodded. "He works very hard."

"Have you talked to Grandma today?" Natalie changed the subject as soon as she could.

There was no point in talking about Christo. There was nothing she could tell her mother—and nothing her mother could say about Christo that she wanted to hear.

She'd got through the last week and a half in zombie-like fashion, putting in time, taking things one at a time, trying to focus on the matter at hand, and ruthlessly dragging her thoughts away from Christo every time they ventured in that direction all day long.

And she had survived.

But the nights nearly did her in. She couldn't sleep. She could only lie there and remember. It was all there to replay endlessly, to make her smile and cringe and laugh and ache.

It would get better, she told herself. She would move on, find new preoccupations.

"Get a life," Sophy had suggested more than once in the past ten days. "Or better yet, take a vacation. You look like death," she'd said this morning when Natalie had been working at the office.

"I do not," Natalie retorted. "I'm fine."

"You have big dark circles under your eyes."

"I'm not sleeping well. I'm…allergic."

"Sure you are," Sophy said. "And I'm the tooth fairy. I told you Savas men can break your heart."

Natalie just looked at her.

Sophy sighed. "I know. It doesn't help being told. You can't help yourself. But honestly, Nat, you should take a few days off. Go away. Get some perspective."

What good perspective would do, Natalie didn't know.

But she said, "I'll think about it." She even considered asking her mother about good places to go. Laura had taken some trips by herself and with friends after Clayton had walked out.

She'd picked up the pieces of her life and made a new one.

She was a perfect role model. Natalie knew she could do worse than emulate her mother.

She *would* emulate her mother.

She just needed a little more time.

She was glad she'd invited her mother to dinner, though

she hedged a bit when Laura suggested they do it again next week at her apartment.

"You come over here," Natalie said, not wanting to risk any chance of seeing Christo. "You almost never come here."

"I'm here now," Laura pointed out. "And if you come to me we can walk on The Strand afterwards. I'm trying to walk at least two miles a day. Part of my keeping-fit regimen."

"Maybe," Natalie said. "I'll see."

But when her mother mentioned it again as she was leaving, Natalie didn't commit herself. "We'll talk about it next week," she said as she walked her mother out to her car.

It was a cool night for early August. It never got especially cool as far inland as Natalie lived. But at the beach it might even be sweater weather. Her mother pulled one on before she got into her car, then turned to give Natalie a kiss.

"Thank you so much for dinner. And for taking care of Herbie—and Christo—while I was gone."

Natalie smiled. "Glad to do it."

"Hope they weren't too much trouble."

Natalie shook her head. "No trouble at all."

Not the cat, anyway. Memories of the man were destroying her peace of mind. But Laura would never ever know that. She would simply believe that Christo had needed help and Natalie had stepped into the breach.

When her mother left, Natalie went back inside and wished she had the table to clear and the dishes to do.

But Laura had insisted on helping her with them. So the kitchen was now spic and span, and Natalie had yet another empty evening stretching in front of her.

If she sat down to read, her mind wandered in directions she didn't want. And if she watched television, it was even worse. She caught up on all her paperwork from Rent-a-

Wife, but it took her no time at all to fill out the online schedule for the rest of the week. She made all the phone calls to confirm tomorrow's assignments, and even rang Sophy to make sure she'd covered everything.

"You need counseling," Sophy told her severely. "Or a ticket to the far ends of the earth."

Natalie didn't reply to that, though there were times the far ends of the earth seemed damned appealing. She just said good-night and hung up, then glanced at her watch, wishing it were later, wishing she were more tired, wishing she would stop having every other thought be about Christo Savas.

The quick sharp rap on her front door came as a welcome surprise.

She didn't know many of her neighbors, but occasionally one appeared needing to borrow sugar or an apple or a blender.

Now she opened the door, eager for the distraction—and stared.

It was Christo.

CHAPTER SEVEN

THE mere sight of him caused her heart to leap, proving that for all that she might have been telling herself that things were getting better and that she was getting over him, the truth was, she wasn't over him in the least.

"Christo?" She gripped the door so hard her fingers hurt.

"I need to talk to you." He didn't smile. He looked, in fact, positively grim.

She didn't want to let him in. It would only be harder when he left again. But she was supposed not to care, she reminded herself. So she stepped back and opened the door wider. "Come in. Sit down."

He came in. He didn't sit down. He cracked his knuckles, paced a bit.

Natalie didn't say anything. He'd sit down if he wanted. He jammed his hands in his pockets and faced her.

"I have a favor to ask. A business proposition, I guess you'd say."

Whatever she'd been expecting, it wasn't that. "Business?"

"Rent-a-Wife," he said. "That's what you do, right? Only I don't need a wife. I need…a fiancée." He met her gaze squarely. "You."

Natalie gaped at him. "I don't think so," she managed before he cut her off.

"Hear me out. My father's getting married." He started to pace a bit again. "To make my grandmother happy."

"What?"

"My grandmother is ill. Dying." He seemed to force the word past his lips, and Natalie could see how shaken he looked as he said it. "She didn't tell me. He did." He sounded angry now. "Called me yesterday and dropped the whole thing on me. Her…illness. His wedding." He raked fingers through his hair. "It's to make her happy."

"His wedding? I'm not sure weddings are supposed to make *other* people happy," she ventured. "Except coincidentally, perhaps."

"Well, it'll make my grandmother happy. She thinks he needs to settle down. So he is." Christo shook his head. "And I have to be there. I'm the 'best man,'" he added, his tone twisting the words derisively.

She could see how much the prospect thrilled him. It was a mockery of everything he professed to believe. But then so was his "business proposal."

"What's the fiancée thing got to do with it?" Natalie asked.

A muscle ticked in his jaw. "Because she wants the same thing for me. Settling down. Marriage." He looked positively hunted. "And if I don't show up with someone in line for exactly that, she'll feel like she has to throw every damn eligible woman in Brazil at me!"

"Let her," Natalie suggested.

"No. She'll want it too much…" His words trailed off, but Natalie thought she understood the implications.

"And you're afraid you'll marry someone to make her happy."

He didn't answer, but she had an inkling of how devoted he was to his grandmother. And if his father was marrying to please her, it wasn't impossible to imagine Christo doing the same.

"If you come with me, I won't have to," he said now.

As if it were up to her to prevent the disaster of matrimony.

"No," Natalie said. "It would be wrong."

"It isn't wrong, damn it!" he countered, eyes blazing. "It's not wrong to want her to have peace of mind."

"It would be a lie."

"We don't have to lie."

"You said you wanted to hire me to be your fiancée! That's a lie."

"Fine. I'll propose. You say yes. And we can call it off when we get back!"

She stared at him, dumbstruck.

He raked a hand through his hair. "Look, it's not a big deal. Just an…arrangement." He took a breath. "We won't lie, then. I'll just bring you along. It will speak for itself." His gaze entreated her.

Natalie hesitated.

"I won't touch you again if that's what you're worried about." His voice was harsh and he jammed his hands into the pockets of his jeans.

Then she did stare. "What?"

"I'm not expecting you to sleep with me. This is not that kind of trip."

"Don't get any ideas, you mean?" Natalie raised a brow.

He shrugged. "You don't have any, do you? Of course you don't. You proved it. That's why I can ask you."

Hoist on her own petard.

"For a week, Nat. That's all. I'll pay you."

Her jaw snapped shut. "You will not *pay* me!"

"Well, it's business. But, fine. I won't. I just…please. You'll make an old—"

"If you say, I'll make an old woman happy, I'll stuff a sock down your throat!"

A corner of his mouth twitched. But he shrugged. "Okay, I won't say it. How about, you'll make me happy?"

"Oh, and I desperately want to make you happy, don't I?" she retorted sarcastically.

He didn't answer, just waited her out. And there wasn't enough time in the world for her to muster enough common sense and self-preservation to say no.

She drew a sharp breath, knowing herself to be a fool. Nothing had changed after all. "Fine," she muttered. "I'll do it. But only because Sophy keeps telling me to take a vacation."

"We leave on Tuesday." Christo grinned, triumphant. But in his eyes Natalie could still see the haunted, worried look beneath it.

He gave her a ring.

They were standing at the airport, waiting to board the plane and all of a sudden he fished in his pocket and took out a small black velvet box.

Natalie stared at it as if it were a rattler about to strike. "What's that?" she demanded, sure it was exactly what she hoped it was not.

Christo flipped open the box. It was. A perfect diamond solitaire. Very spare and elegant. Not a rock, but not minuscule either. Exactly the sort of ring Christo would give a woman he was going to marry—if Christo were going to marry anyone. Which he wasn't.

"You said we weren't going to lie!"

"It's not a lie."

"What? It's a prop?"

He shrugged. "If you will, yes." He looked exasperated. "Look. Just wear it, will you? Consider it part of the uniform."

He held it out to put on her finger, and she scowled, but finally stuck her hand out. "It probably won't fit anyway," she muttered. She had big hands, not the delicate ones men always seemed to expect.

"It will," Christo said confidently.

And damn it, he was right. It slid on and fit perfectly. Natalie stared at the ring glittering on her finger and felt a sinking desperation somewhere deep inside. She started to tremble.

"How did you—?" she began, but couldn't even finish.

"I asked your mother your ring size."

Her gaze jerked up and she stared at him, horrified. "You asked my *mother?* What size *ring* I wear? Are you crazy? What on earth will she think?" Oh, God. It didn't even bear thinking about!

"What will she think? The truth. She asked, and I told her the truth."

"That you were hiring me to be your...fiancée?"

He shrugged. "She knows about my grandmother. She's met her. She understood."

She did? And what had she thought about Natalie being his choice for fake fiancée? Had she wondered why? If so, she hadn't asked.

She hadn't called her daughter, either, though Natalie couldn't quite imagine her mother being as sanguine as Christo thought she was. But then, she had to have known since at least yesterday for him to have bought a ring. And Laura hadn't called and tried to talk her out of it.

Was her mother expecting something to come of it? Dear God, what a mess.

"This is going to be a disaster," Natalie said with quiet certainty.

"No, it won't," Christo said. "It will be fine. It has to be fine," he added fiercely.

The line was moving now. They were edging toward the plane, and as they moved, Natalie twisted the ring on her finger and was excruciatingly aware of Christo's hand lightly touching her back.

It was easy to spot Lucia Azevedo when they'd reached the baggage-claim area. She was the small, birdlike woman whose pale face simply lit up at the sight of Christo. She crossed the space that separated them in seconds and wrapped Christo in a fierce hug, then stepped back to regard Natalie with an intent gaze.

"So you are my Christo's lady?" Her voice was a bit reserved as she offered her hand, which Natalie took. Her fingers were thin and bony, but warm, and Natalie felt determined strength in them as they pressed hers.

"I'm so happy to meet you, Senhora Azevedo," Natalie said, and though she felt a twinge of guilt at the way she was doing it, she meant every word. Ever since she'd heard the stories Christo had told Jamii, she had wanted to meet this woman who meant so much to him.

"Call me Lucia," his grandmother said.

"Lucia," Natalie repeated dutifully. "Thank you for inviting me. And thank you, Senhor Azevedo," she said to the man who stood fidgeting in the background.

He had stayed back until his mother had finished greeting Christo and Natalie, as if he knew who really mattered to Christo. But now he embraced his son and clapped him on the back, then kissed Natalie on both cheeks.

"Xanti," he corrected her. "*Senhor* Azevedo makes me sound like my father. Dead."

"Beloved," his mother corrected firmly, slapping his arm lightly. "And deeply missed."

"*Sim.* And not replaceable. So I am Xanti," her son said just as firmly, taking her hand in his.

Xantiago Azevedo was in his mid fifties now, but unlike many men his age he had retained the lithe, lean, soccer player's build he must have had in his prime. He wasn't as broad-shouldered as Christo, nor as handsome in Natalie's estimation, but she could see instantly that Xanti's quicksilver grin would always have appealed to the ladies. And there was a twinkle in his green eyes, which were much more devilish than his serious son's.

"Where's Katia?" Christo asked his father now.

Katia was the bride. But more than that Natalie hadn't discovered.

"I've met her once or twice," Christo had said. "She's young. Beautiful. The sort Xanti always goes for. Not much older than me." There was a mixture of doubt and censure in his tone. He looked around now, but apparently didn't see her. He looked quizzically at his father.

Xanti laughed and shrugged. "Running around like a chicken," he said, shaking his head as he hoisted one of the suitcases Christo had taken off the luggage turntable and led the way out the door. "She has so much to do before the wedding. Me, I don't know what is so important."

"I know," his mother said imperiously. "The wedding is important. She wants it to be perfect."

Christo rolled his eyes at that comment, but fortunately his grandmother didn't see him. She was focused on walking as they went out of the terminal. Her gait was slow and not terribly steady. Natalie slowed her pace to match and offered Christo's grandmother her arm for support.

"Maybe your father could bring the car and meet your grandmother and me here?" she called to Christo who, laden with two more suitcases, had been going after his father.

He glanced back, realized at once what she meant, and called something to his father in Portuguese. Then he immediately turned back and helped Natalie usher his grandmother to a bench.

"You shouldn't have come," he scolded her. "You should have stayed home to rest."

She looked indignant as she sank onto the seat. "For what do I rest? For you. You are here at last. Who knows how many days I have to see you?"

"Don't say things like that," Christo chastised her roughly.

His grandmother shrugged. "It is true." And she looked up at him with such love that it was almost painful to watch—especially since Natalie had a very good idea how she felt.

It took over an hour to get to the house that Xanti had built for his mother after he'd become an international soccer star. It was in the same rural area he had grown up in, with a mixture of working farms and large estates. And when they arrived, Natalie realized that it wasn't simply a house, but a small compound of two good-sized houses and several smaller cottages.

"Because Xanti wanted home-cooked meals, but he didn't want Avó telling him not to bring his women home,"

Christo explained wryly after they'd taken his grandmother to her house and she'd been persuaded to take a short rest. "She has her place here and he has his over there—" a wave of the hand toward a sprawling modern place near a free-form landscaped swimming pool. "And there are others for family and visitors," he added as he walked her through the beautiful grounds along a winding flagstone path that ended at the door of a small cottage. "This one is for you."

The one he'd brought her to was older than the others, a rough ivory-colored stucco house with deep-set windows and a broad flagstone veranda all across the front. It was quite the most lovely welcoming little house Natalie had ever seen.

On a trellis on one side of the porch a deep burgundy bougainvillea grew all the way up to the roof and draped along it, providing privacy and welcome shade from the sun.

Though it was winter in Brazil, the day was still warm, and Natalie was glad to step into the shade while Christo took out a key and opened the door, then held it for her to precede him.

The inside of the house was cool and as welcoming at the exterior. A rattan sofa and chairs with colorful jungle print cushions were grouped at one end of the main room, and there was a small kitchen and dining area at the other. French doors opened onto another veranda beyond the dining table.

There was a small hallway with a bath and a bedroom where Christo carried her suitcase. Natalie followed him in and stopped as she stared at the one wide bed.

Instantly her gaze flew to Christo at the same moment he turned and looked at her.

"I'm staying at Avó's," he said. "Don't worry. You can, too, of course. I just thought, under the circumstances, you

might prefer it here where you could have a little privacy
and some space. Where you won't be under the microscope
all the time."

"I would," Natalie said quickly. "Thank you."

She smiled at him then, and for the first time since she'd
agreed to come, it felt almost right. Almost as if she might
not have made the biggest mistake of her life.

Walking back out into the main room, she turned in a
circle, trying to absorb the peace and the beauty of the
place. "It's gorgeous here, all of it," she told Christo. "Your
dad's place looks amazing and your grandmother's is really
lovely. But I really like it here best. It's homey."

She wondered, when she said it, if it sounded rude. But
for the first time Christo actually smiled, too.

"It was Avó's," he told her. "This is her old house.
Renovated a bit now—" he nodded toward the updated
kitchen "—but it was where she and my grandfather lived,
where Xanti was raised. It was where she was still living
when I first came here as a boy. Xanti was living in Europe
then. Making lots of money, but he hadn't come back yet
to build his palace." He dipped his head in the direction of
Xanti's house, then looked around here and ran his hand
down the doorjamb proprietarily. "I like it here, too."

It was one of those moments of perfect communion that
they shared. One that made Natalie ache with longing for
what could be but never would. What it made Christo feel,
she didn't know.

Abruptly he said, "I should go back and see Avó. Do you
want to come or will you rest a while?"

"I'll rest," Natalie said.

He opened his mouth, started to say something, then
shut it again. Another long look arced between them, and

Natalie found herself almost leaning into it before she recollected herself and straightened up.

Christo ran his tongue over his lips, then cleared his throat. "Come up to Avó's when you feel like it," he said, businesslike again, already stepping toward the door. *"Tchau."*

"Tchau," Natalie whispered and felt her throat close on the word.

But Christo didn't hear. He was already striding toward his grandmother's house, not even glancing back.

It had been the right thing to bring Natalie.

It was important for his grandmother not to worry about him. And she would have worried, even though she would have smiled and teased and made a joke of throwing women in his way.

Christo had been shocked at the change in her. He'd seen her four months ago when he'd come to visit over Easter. And she was a shadow now of the woman she'd been then.

He hadn't believed his father when he'd called. Had it been only five days ago? Yes. It didn't seem possible for the world to have changed that fast. Maybe the whole world hadn't, but his had.

His grandmother had been the single constant dependable anchor in his life since he'd been barely six years old. She was the one who'd had time for him, who'd listened to him, who'd both trusted him and demanded more of him. The man he'd become owed more to her than to anyone.

He hadn't believed it when Xanti had said she was dying.

"I just talked to her a couple of weeks ago!" Christo had protested. "She never said a word."

"Would she?"

The question had stopped Christo's protest like a blow to the heart.

Would she tell him? He knew the answer even as his father's question echoed in his head.

No, she wouldn't. Not while he was so far away. Not while he had his own life. She wouldn't want to take him away from it, wouldn't want him to worry, to fret about what he couldn't change.

But now that he thought about it, he remembered again the talk about finding him a wife. There had been gentle teasing in her words as there always was. But last time there had been something urgent. Something more.

"She is dying," Xanti repeated. "So I'm getting married."

"To whom?" Christo had demanded, stunned.

"To Katia! Who else?" Xanti had sounded affronted at the question. Katia Ferreira did public relations for the sporting-goods company his father worked with. She was in her mid-thirties, pretty enough, very blonde, a quick-witted, savvy businesswoman. Unlike the other women who had come and gone in his father's life, Katia had never seemed enthralled by Xanti's boyish antics and mercurial behavior—or by Xanti himself for that matter.

"And she'll have you?" Christo had asked.

"She loves me. It will be good," Xanti retorted. "It will make your grandmother happy. She can stop worrying about me."

Ergo, Christo knew, she would be worrying about him. About finding a wife for him. And that had led him instinctively to the notion of bringing Natalie with him to Brazil.

But the moment he'd thought it, he knew he couldn't. Then he knew he had to. He didn't want to. Oh, yes, he did.

His mind, usually incisive, his decisions, clear-cut, were

anything but for the next twenty-four hours. It was madness, foolishness. It was a bad idea all around.

But it wouldn't go away. He couldn't ask just any woman, he knew that. Avó wasn't stupid. She would see through such a ruse in a minute.

But she would believe Natalie.

She would *love* Natalie.

She wouldn't just see the outer beauty of Natalie Ross. She would appreciate her gentleness, her compassion, her innate toughness, her sincerity, her sense of humor. They were both strong people, caring people.

He suspected Natalie would like his grandmother, too.

But it hadn't been easy to ask her. He still thought about her far too often. He still woke up reaching for her.

Besides, he knew she'd object. He knew she'd say it was wrong.

It wasn't, damn it. Not to make the most beloved person in his life happy. Not to keep her from worrying about something she had no control over.

But if he thought the asking had been hard, having Natalie here with him now in the bosom of his family was worse—because almost instantly she seemed to belong.

The days were busy with wedding preparations. He didn't have a lot of time to spend with her because Xanti was always thinking of things to have him do.

"Don't worry. I'm fine," she said when he apologized. "I can help, too."

She did—running errands for Katia, making place cards for the tables at the reception, even helping with some minor alterations to the wedding dress. And if she spent a fair amount of time helping Katia, she spent even more time with his grandmother.

Despite her discomfort with their charade, she played it well. She didn't keep a low profile. And she didn't shy away from his family.

On the contrary, she sought them out.

"You don't have to spend every minute with them," he told her.

She looked at him, her eyes wide and hurt. "Would you rather I didn't?"

"Of course not. It's fine," he said gruffly, scowling, out of sorts and not quite sure why. "I just don't want you to feel—put upon."

"I'm not. I'm enjoying myself. I like your grandmother."

"She likes you, too."

So did everyone else.

Xanti, of course, thought she was delightful. But Xanti thought that about most females. There was more to his approval of Natalie, though.

Thursday night, two days after they'd arrived, he and his father were sharing a beer on the veranda and staying out of the way of even more wedding preparations going on in Avó's house. They stood there in the twilight and watched through the windows as the women bustled back and forth.

Then Xanti dropped into a chair and tipped it back on two legs, then took a long swallow of his beer and looked up at his son who leaned against one of the uprights that supported the veranda roof. "You're a lot smarter than I was at your age."

Christo raised a brow. "Doesn't take much."

Xanti laughed. "Probably not. Some men teach by bad example. And I did a damn good job of it for a lot of years." Then his grin faded and his expression grew serious as he added, "But I'm glad you didn't turn out the same way. Glad you picked the right woman the first time around."

Christo opened his mouth —and closed it again. He couldn't deny it, so he didn't say anything at all. Only when Xanti looked at him quizzically, did he finally answer.

"I'm glad you approve."

"I do." Xanti was emphatic. "I like Natalie. She makes you smile, brings you to life—the same way Katia settles me down."

That perception did raise Christo's eyebrows. He would not have expected such self-awareness from his father. The first was a variation on a long-standing complaint Xanti had voiced since he was a child—that Christo was always too serious, too adult.

"Someone had to be," had always been Christo's retort.

"I know what you're going to say," Xanti said now, his mouth quirking once more into a faint grin. "And you're right, of course. I wasn't much of a father. I'm sorry. Maybe I'll do better this time around."

"This time?" Christo stared, nonplussed. "You mean—? Is Katia—?" He was speechless at the unspoken possibility Xanti hinted at, though he supposed he shouldn't be.

"No!" Xanti said hastily. "But—" he shrugged fatalistically "—you never know the future, do you? What will be will be, they say. And what about your future? When are you tying the knot?"

Christo, distracted by the possibility of his father becoming one again, dragged his mind back to the question, and realized it was another he didn't want to answer. "We haven't discussed it."

"Why not?"

Christo shrugged his back against one of the uprights of the veranda. "It's early days yet."

"Not as early as you think," Xanti warned. "Don't waste time. Don't string her along."

"Don't give me advice on women," Christo snapped.

All four legs of Xanti's chair came back to earth with a thump. "Relax." He held up a hand as if to back Christo off. "Just offering a suggestion. I'm only saying that your Natalie is too good to lose. You don't want her marrying someone else."

Christo's teeth came together. "She isn't marrying anyone else!"

"Of course not," Xanti said easily. He tipped back again, sipped his beer, stared into the distance.

And Christo tried to breathe again. Tried not to think that someday, of course, she would marry someone else.

She might say she had no intention of ever marrying, but he knew better. Natalie was too loving, too giving. She would find a man to love and she would marry him. Even now he could see her in his grandmother's kitchen, laughing with one of Katia's cousins. One of her *male* cousins.

Primitive feelings of a rage that he didn't want to examine too closely bubbled very near the surface, playing havoc with his common sense and reason. His fingers choked the beer bottle in his hand.

"So," Xanti said, "how about a game of pool?"

"No," Christo said. He shoved away from the upright and thumped his empty beer bottle on the table. "Natalie and I are going for a walk. She wants to see the gardens."

CHAPTER EIGHT

SHE didn't see him coming.

One minute she was busy tying ribbons on little personal boxes of chocolates that Katia had decided would be perfect by each table setting at the reception while she chatted and laughed with Katia's cousin, Julio, who was barely twenty but capable of flirting madly because she was out of reach. And the next Christo was standing at her elbow, saying, "Come out with me."

"You can't take her," Katia protested, laughing. "She's working."

But Christo just said, "She's worked enough. Come on." And giving her no time to object, he took the ribbons out of her hands and hauled her to her feet, practically stepping on Julio's as he did so.

"Boa noite," he said to the whole room, cupping her elbow with his fingers and steering her toward the door.

"Um, *boa noite,*" Natalie echoed as he shut the door behind them. "Good night."

A flurry of *tchaus* and *boa noites* followed them, but Christo kept moving until Natalie dug in her heels and made him stop.

"What," she demanded turning to face him, "was that all about?"

Christo sucked in a sharp breath. His jaw tightened. "I don't know."

She stared at him. "You don't know?"

"I didn't bring you here to work for Katia." He turned and began walking quickly across the lawn toward the gardens.

Natalie hurried to catch up with him. "No, you brought me here to try to convince them we're getting married. And being a part of the family, helping out, is a way to do that."

He jammed his hands in his pockets, but he didn't stop walking. "I know that." He didn't sound angry, but there was an impatient edge to his voice that she was used to hearing only when he was dealing with annoying legal cases and difficult clients.

"So what's the problem? Am I doing something you don't want me to do?"

He opened his mouth, then shut it again abruptly. "No. It's fine. You're doing everything right."

"Yes, I can tell. You're so pleased," she said sarcastically.

His jaw worked, but he didn't say anything. They'd reached the patio with its inground naturally landscaped swimming pool. Lit from below, it gleamed like a bright turquoise gem in the growing darkness. Earlier that afternoon they had swum there, had laughed and teased and splashed water at each other while his grandmother had looked on, smiling. Now that seemed like a hundred years ago.

Just as the nights she had spent in his bed now seemed to have taken place in another lifetime.

The awareness was still there. She could feel it. It seemed to pulse between them even now. In the cool of the evening, she could feel the heat of his presence, though he wasn't even looking at her. Instead he started walking again, heading off down one of the several paths lit with small inground lights that led through small copses and wooded areas.

"Where are we going?" she asked him as she tried to keep up with his long strides.

"To see the gardens."

"Now?" She knew they were on the other side of the woods. His grandmother had talked about them this afternoon, had said that his grandfather had begun them when this was still a farm.

Now Christo turned an impatient scowl on her. "You said you wanted to see them."

"Well, yes. But maybe in the daylight? When they're actually visible?"

He looked startled, as if it hadn't occurred to him.

"Just a thought," she added, tilting her head to give him a tiny smile.

He grimaced, then let out a harsh sigh and raked his fingers through his hair. "Hell."

She put a hand on his arm. It jerked beneath her touch. "What's wrong?"

He shook his head and stepped away, tucking his hand into his pocket again. "Nothing. Xanti ticked me off. He does that. I should know better. I just— Never mind." He shrugged, his tone dismissive now, as if whatever had bothered him, he'd stuffed back into whatever box he kept it in. "Come on. I'll take you back."

"We could just…walk?" she suggested, suddenly reluctant to end their brief interlude of togetherness. They'd had very little since they'd been here.

He hesitated, then shrugged. "All right."

So they walked. Christo knew the land like the back of his hand. He didn't need the tiny lights that picked out the pathway. Natalie would have, but before they had walked a few yards, she felt his hand wrap hers. Their fingers laced in silence. Their shoulders brushed.

Mostly they walked without speaking. What Christo was thinking about, she didn't know. What she was thinking was how badly she wanted this to be real, how much she wanted Christo to stop and turn and take her in his arms and say, "I want this. I want you. I love you."

She trembled with the need that coursed through her.

"Are you cold?" His voice broke into her fantasy. "You should have a sweater."

"I'm all right." But she trembled all the same.

"No, you're not. We'll go back." He'd already turned and, because he still held her hand, Natalie had to turn, too.

He walked more quickly now, purposefully, and in just a few minutes they reached her cottage. He opened the door for her, but he didn't come in.

"Would you like to—?" She waved a hand in the direction of the sofa, offering him a seat.

"I should get back." Their eyes met for a mere instant and awareness, as always, arced between them. She wanted him to forget his vow, wanted him to come to her bed.

"Christo—"

"Good night, Nat." His voice was strained, and he turned on his heel and headed back toward his grandmother's place before she could say another word.

It was just as well, Natalie told herself. She was better off keeping things on a business footing. And that's what this was—business.

But as she shut the door and leaned back against it,

aching with the need of him, she knew the biggest lie she was telling this week was to herself.

Lucia Azevedo might have been frail and ill, but she was no fool.

She had been hospitable and accepting enough of Natalie upon her arrival. But at the same time, there had, understandably, been a bit of reserve in her demeanor.

Natalie had almost been able to see Christo's grandmother looking at her and hear her thinking, *Who is this woman? What's she really like? Do I dare believe she will love my grandson the way he deserves to be loved?*

She didn't come right out and ask, of course. She simply smiled and watched and listened. She spent time with Natalie while everyone else was busy running themselves ragged getting ready for the wedding.

Natalie helped willingly and discovered that every time she did so, Lucia was there, too, watching, listening, occasionally talking if Natalie asked questions.

And despite knowing that emotionally she would likely be far better off not learning everything she could about Christo's life in Brazil, Natalie couldn't help herself.

She asked about the summers he spent there. She was eager to spend hours poring over the pictures Lucia was very happy to show her and she loved to listen to the tales Lucia told about the solemn, silent little boy who had come to visit her and who had grown into the strong and caring man who was the Christo she knew.

"He was such a serious little boy," Lucia said fondly, shaking her head at the memory. They were sitting on the patio watching Christo kick a soccer ball around with his father. "He didn't know how to play. At least I think Xanti taught him that—" She nodded now at Christo laughing at something his father said, then dribbling the ball past Xanti's outstretched foot. "But really, Christo was always the adult."

Natalie wasn't surprised at the image. Xanti was far more playful and flirtatious than his son.

"Of course he had to be," Christo's grandmother went on. "He always felt he had to keep things together. He'd been taking care of his mother for most of his life, it seems, and when at last she and Xanti married, I think he believed he could start being a child. But things just got worse."

Natalie raised her brows. "Worse?"

Lucia nodded. "Such children they were, those two. Squabbling, fighting. Each wanting their own way. It was better when Christo was here. He could be a child here."

Natalie had a million questions about the little boy Christo had been, but she didn't ask. She waited, hoping that Lucia would share, and was rewarded when she did.

"That first time was hard for him. Xanti, of course, didn't stay around. He just left Christo with me and went on his merry way back to Italy. Christo didn't know what to do, what to think. He didn't speak the language. He didn't know me. But—" she smiled at the memory "—we worked it out. He knew how to get along. He thought I might keep him if he made himself useful." Another smile. "So he did. And he worked at learning Portuguese. I admired him for it. I learned English because of him. We taught each other."

"You are the most important person in his life," Natalie said.

"I was," Lucia agreed. "Now it is you."

"Not really. I—"

But Lucia cut her off gently but firmly. "And that is how it should be." She reached out and patted Natalie's hand.

"He is still too solemn sometimes," his grandmother said. "Still very, what do you say? Self-contained? He is hard to know, *sim?*" She slanted a glance at Natalie who nodded. Lucia smiled. "So I think you have great powers to get inside his walls."

Natalie swallowed the lump in her throat. "I love him."

Lucia tilted her head. Her gaze rested on Natalie a long moment—so long that Natalie knew how a bug under a microscope felt. But she didn't flinch away. It was only the truth.

Whatever Lucia saw, at last she, too, nodded. *"Sim,"* she said gently and reached out to take Natalie's fingers between hers. "I believe you do."

Her smile changed then. It had always been a polite smile, a welcoming smile. But now it reached her eyes. And in them Natalie saw a love that embraced not only Christo, but her as well as she leaned across and touched soft lips to Natalie's cheek.

"You don't know how happy you have made me." Her voice was husky with emotion. "I was so afraid Christo would never find a woman who would capture his heart."

What was Natalie supposed to say to that? *I haven't? I love him but he's only hired me to be his fiancée for the week?*

Of course, she couldn't say that—or anything remotely like it. She could only squeeze his grandmother's fingers lightly and smile.

"It is time he let down his defenses." Lucia went on approvingly. "He is very well-defended, you know."

"I know."

"He must trust you very much."

"I hope so." Maybe he didn't love her, but she thought

he did trust her. He wouldn't have brought her if he hadn't. She glanced over at him and found that he was looking at her as well.

After one more kick, he left his father dribbling the ball and jogged over to them, his gaze moving from Natalie's face to her fingers clasped with his grandmother's. He raised his brows.

"Telling secrets?" he said to his grandmother with a smile.

"Of course." She laughed lightly and patted Natalie's hand. Then she shook her head. "I am simply telling your Natalie how happy I am that you have found the woman of your heart."

Something unreadable flickered in his gaze for a brief instant. But then he smiled. "Of course I have," he said smoothly, and bent to drop a light kiss on Natalie's lips.

It was an act. Natalie knew that. Of course it was no hardship to kiss her, but he didn't mean anything by it. But even so, after he went back to the soccer ball and his father, she couldn't help touching her lips and holding the memory in her heart.

"Where did you meet my Christo?" Lucia asked her.

"When I was interning at the firm he worked for." She told the truth as far as she could—about how she'd met him that first time, and how she'd fallen for him—on looks alone—without really even knowing him. But then she said she'd got to know him better, but she'd only come to appreciate what a good man he was later that summer.

She didn't say how she'd figured that out. Telling Lucia that she'd gone to Christo's bed and he'd turned her down was a bit more truth than she could bring herself to share.

Then she told Lucia about the time she'd spent at her mother's where she'd met him again. She told her about his kindness to Jamii, about his getting Jamii to go in the water by telling her about when he'd been able to get over his fear of heights after falling.

"Because you helped him," she told Lucia.

His grandmother laughed. "I was terrified. I hate heights. But for Christo—well, sometimes you have to do things that you're afraid of, don't you? I love him. You know how that is. You are Christo's lady."

Natalie knew how it was, oh yes. Just as she knew that she was not really Christo's lady.

The wedding took place just before sunset in the garden between Xanti's house and Lucia's. Natalie sat next to Christo's grandmother, her fingers firmly entwined in the older woman's as Xanti, looking surprisingly pale and nervous, and Christo, his best man, looking more serious and remote than ever, stood waiting for the bride and her attendants to walk down the path to join them.

It was a tableau to memorize and keep in her heart—father and son together, so alike in their dark suits, crisp white shirts and neat bow ties. Yet, after a moment, Natalie had eyes only for one. She could have sat there and simply drunk in the sight of Christo forever.

He was the most handsome man she'd ever seen. Taller and broader-shouldered than his father. Less fidgety, too. Xanti kept running his finger inside the collar of his starched shirt. Christo didn't move a muscle, not even when the quintet began to play and the guests turned to watch the first of the bridesmaids come down the path.

Then, because everyone else did, Natalie turned to watch the procession as well. There were three bridesmaids, followed by a resplendent Katia, who was a beautiful bride.

In a short, simple, understated dress of ivory silk, she looked regal and serene and steady as she approached Xanti. He still had the look of a rabbit caught in headlights. But when at last Katia reached him and put her hand in his, he swallowed hard, his color seemed to return. And in his eyes when he looked at his bride, Natalie could see that despite his nerves, despite his mercurial personality, despite everything—Xanti was exactly where he wanted to be.

As they stood together and the ceremony began, Natalie found that she didn't need to speak Portuguese to understand. While Katia's gentle voice and Xanti's gruffer one might repeat words she didn't recognize, the sentiments expressed and the vows taken were crystal-clear.

The familiar form and expectations provided a sort of anchor for her to hang on to in the dangerous sea of her current emotions.

A very dangerous anchor, Natalie knew.

It gave her unrealistic ideas. It drew her eyes away from the bride and groom to study Christo again, to allow herself to imagine what it would be like to be marrying him.

Would he look worried and nervous, as his father did? Would he smile? Could he ever wear the same look of love that Xanti had worn?

None of the above, she reminded herself sharply.

Thinking about Christo and marriage in the same sentence was the quickest way imaginable to a broken heart.

As if she wouldn't have one anyway by the time this way over.

Deliberately, Natalie forced her gaze away, focusing once more on the radiant bride and the still-nervous groom who fumbled the ring when Christo handed it to him and nearly dropped it before he got it on Katia's finger.

But the moment the celebrant pronounced them man and wife, Xanti kissed his bride triumphantly, and suddenly he was a new man. He turned to face the guests, grinning broadly and clutching Katia's hands in his. And the expression on his face told them that they were looking at the happiest man on earth.

Next to Natalie, Lucia was wiping tears from her eyes and smiling radiantly. Everyone was—laughing, cheering and applauding the new Senhor *e* Senhora Xantiago Azevedo.

Everyone except Christo, who stood staring into the middle distance, stone-faced and remote. He might have been a million miles away, Natalie thought. And doubtless wished he were.

The determined indifference of his gaze was so at odds with his father's and grandmother's and, indeed, everyone else's, that Natalie couldn't look away—not even when, for a brief moment, his eyes met hers. His gaze was dark and unreadable.

Natalie hoped the longing didn't show in hers.

If he detected it, she didn't know. But barely a second passed before he looked away. Then it was his turn to offer his arm to the maid of honor so they could follow Xanti and Katia up the path together.

The immense rambling garden had been hung with thousands of twinkling white fairy lights for the reception immediately following. It looked like a magical world. And as the sun set it took on an even more bewitching aura.

The verandas outside Xanti's house and his mother's had each been set with groups of tables for a casually elegant catered meal. At many of the weddings Natalie had attended the wedding party ate at their own table. But here they mingled with the guests and she was seated next to Christo.

"Where else?" his grandmother had said when Natalie expressed her surprise. "It is the right place for you."

It was certainly the right place to make Natalie even more aware of him than she was already.

Maybe it was because they were at a wedding. Maybe it was the determined restraint he'd shown all week, even as unacknowledged desire still hummed between them. Maybe it was simply her heightened awareness of how short the time was growing when she would still have him in her life.

But as they sat next to each other at dinner, she was aware the instant that the elbow of his suit jacket brushed against her arm when he cut his meat. When he gave the toast to his father and Katia, then touched his champagne glass to hers, their fingers touched, and both of them seemed to jerk as if electricity had arced between them.

As they stood together after the meal, casually he slipped an arm around her shoulders, as any good fiancé would do. But Natalie sensed it the second his fingers twined in her hair.

He didn't have to do that, did he?

No. He wanted to do it. And she wanted him to. She couldn't help sidestepping to bring them just a little bit closer so that her hip rested against his as he talked to a couple of his cousins.

She was just being a good fiancée. That was all. Christo could have stepped away. He didn't.

He turned his head and she felt his breath stir the tendrils of hair by her ear. It sent a frisson of longing through her. Emboldened by her desire, she slid an arm around his waist and felt his body stiffen.

But still he didn't let go. If anything, his grip on her tightened. He held her fast to his side—exactly where she wanted to be.

Tomorrow it would be all over. They would fly home and go their separate ways. Natalie knew that. Accepted it.

But tonight?

She swallowed. Faced the reality of her desire and knew that tonight she would take her touches where she could get them. And to hell with the consequences.

Christo let his fingers play with her hair while he talked to his cousin Marcelo. It wasn't much of an indulgence. Not even close to what he wanted to do. But it was something a fiancé would do at his father's wedding, and so Christo allowed himself to do it.

He hadn't allowed himself much all week.

A kiss here. A touch there. A little bit of public hand-holding. Just enough, he assured himself, so that Avó would believe. Not so much that he would lose his sanity and common sense.

Now Natalie laughed at something his cousin Breno was saying. She shifted her weight slightly and he felt her hip press against his. He swallowed. Drew in a slow breath.

He could have stepped away. He didn't. It was only a for moment, after all.

Then the breeze lifted her hair and blew a strand toward him, and he turned into it, let it trail across his face, breathing in the scent of her shampoo.

It was one that he knew he would never forget. The hint of fresh lime and coconut might once have reminded him of summers at the beach. Now they brought back the nights Natalie had spent in his arms.

He itched to pull her into them again. The arm that he had slung over her shoulder instinctively drew her just a little closer and he felt her body mold itself against his side.

She leaned her head against his shoulder and her cheek rubbed against the light wool of his jacket.

He knew how soft the skin on that cheek was. He wanted once more to feel that softness rub against his whisker-stubbled one, wanted to brush his lips against it and—

"Christo! *Vem!* Time to dance." His father's voice jerked him out of his reverie.

"Dance?" Christo echoed, then remembered that his duties as best man hadn't quite ended.

"One dance with my maid of honor," Katia had told him yesterday at the rehearsal. At his pained look, she'd patted his cheek. "Just one. And then you can dance all night with your Natalie."

Dance all night with Natalie? And keep his hands off her afterwards? How much of a saint did Katia think he was?

Probably she didn't think he was a saint at all. Probably she thought he'd do exactly what he wanted to do.

Christo drew back sharply and let go of Natalie. "I have to find Amelia," he said abruptly, started away, then realized he wasn't acting as quite a doting fiancé as he ought. "You'll be all right with Breno and Marcelo?"

She nodded. "I'll be fine."

Of course she would. It was why he'd brought her, after all. She had done everything he'd wanted her to do.

He went in search of Amelia, a tall, svelte, dark-haired beauty, single and, judging from the looks she'd been giving him, quite likely available.

The music started and he spun her into his arms and focused on the dance. The woman didn't interest him.

Only one woman interested him. And she was "fine" right where she was, on the other side of the dance floor, tapping her toe in time with the quick beat of music.

Her gaze was on him. He could feel it. Could feel her eyes follow him as he moved. He could almost feel them physically—as if her fingertips were outlining the curve of his ear, caressing the nape of his neck, heating his body, boiling his blood.

Amelia murmured something. He didn't hear her. Didn't look at her. His eyes were solely on Natalie across the floor while he danced easily, almost instinctively. Avó had taught him how when he was only a child.

"Feel the rhythm," she would say. "Let it carry you like the waves."

He'd given himself over to it then, let it carry him, make him part of it. The rhythm became his nature. It pounded in his blood.

So did Natalie.

In his arms he had Amelia, in his mind, in his heart, he danced with Natalie. God knew he wanted to.

God also knew what would happen if he did.

So he didn't. He didn't dare.

Natalie wasn't much of a dancer. She moved with music, but rarely outside the privacy of her apartment. She tended more often to sit on the sidelines, as she was doing tonight, and admire those who could do it and do it well. She'd never wanted to be one of them.

Until she saw Christo on the dance floor.

Watching his body move with such primal grace in unison with another body made her wish the body was hers. Of course she would never be as accomplished as Katia's bridesmaid. She would never move so easily, so beautifully as the woman in Christo's arms.

But once she had, she realized. In fact, more than once.

When she'd made love with Christo, they'd moved together. Their bodies had meshed. She had danced with him in his bed.

She had known him with a deeper intimacy than this woman ever could.

Now, watching, unable to take her eyes off him, she desperately wanted to again. Surely he would come to her. When the music ended, so did his obligation to Amelia.

Breno, following her gaze, said, "Don't worry. He's got one duty dance, then he's all yours."

But when the dance was over and a new one began, he didn't come to her. It was a slow dance, wistful, romantic—perfect for a fool like her, Natalie thought as she watched him cross the floor and reach his grandmother's side, hold out his hand to her, draw her to her feet.

Of course, Natalie thought, smiling at the rightness of it as Christo led Lucia to the floor and took her small frail body so gently in his arms. Her eyes pricked with tears as she watched them, saw them dance together slowly, saw them sway to the rhythm together, so in tune with each other.

She saw Lucia turn her face up and smile into Christo's, and saw his face light with rare tenderness as he said something in reply. He had lost his grim distant expression at last.

He was in the moment. He was where he ought to be. He had made his grandmother happy—exactly as he'd wanted to do.

When the music ended he took his grandmother back to her table and sat down with her.

A fast lilting tune filled the air, Xanti and Katia led the dance and eager couples headed to the floor again. But Christo stayed with his grandmother, not even glancing Natalie's way.

"Dance with me?" Breno said, giving her a wink and a smile. He held out his hand.

"I'm not very good," Natalie objected.

"I am," Breno winked at her. "*Vem.* Come." There was a hint of the imperiousness of his cousin, but Breno was more a flirtatious charmer. He grasped her hand and spun her with him onto the floor.

He moved fluidly, grinning broadly as he drew her with him, leading her easily, spinning her, moving her as efficiently as if she were a rag doll with no bones and no brains of her own.

It was dizzying, crazy, and she was moving too quickly to catch more than a glimpse of Christo with his grandmother. For a second she did and then Breno spun her away again. He made her laugh with exhilaration when he twirled her like a top. And at the music's end he gave her one last spin so she was flung back dramatically in his arms.

"Not very good?" Breno raised his brows doubtfully as he drew her upright again. "Again?" he asked as the music began again.

"Não." Christo's voice came from behind her, hard and precise. "This one is mine."

He took her hand in his and drew her hard against him, her knees banged against his knees, her breasts pressed against his chest. She thought there was a telltale hardness south of his belt and moved against him to be sure. He gritted his teeth.

Natalie looked up at him, relished the feel of him, moved closer still. "We danced in your bed," she said as they began to move together with the music.

Something almost primal flashed in his eyes as he

looked at her. Their gazes held for a long moment, then he bent his head closer.

"And now we're dancing here." His voice was almost a growl in her ear.

Dancing? Or making love?

Both, Natalie thought as the music wrapped them in its spell.

Breno had been a good dancer. It had been easy to follow his lead. But with Christo, she followed not just his body, but her heart.

He could lead her anywhere and she would follow. She had come here, hadn't she? Done his bidding? Set herself up for a lifetime of pain?

His fingers pressed against her back, melding them ever closer.

"I want you." Christo's voice was ragged against her cheek. "I can't take this anymore. When this is over, I want you. Tonight."

They were words she'd despaired of ever hearing again. Words that made her heart sing. And even the word *tonight* didn't daunt her. She wasn't asking for forever.

She turned her head to touch her lips to his. "Yes," she whispered. "Oh, yes."

CHAPTER NINE

CHRISTO walked her back to her cottage wordlessly. His hand at the small of her back seemed to burn right through to her skin. And he was close enough that the heat from his body—and hers—seemed to simmer between them. The music was still playing, moody and romantic now. There was no pounding beat. It didn't matter. Desire was still humming through the warm and humid air.

Jungle air, she had heard Christo call it.

"The sort of air that makes savages of us all," Xanti had said tonight with a wink in the direction of his bride. And then he'd said gruffly, "Savages—or lovers."

"Or grooms," his bride had countered to the laughter of all assembled. And Xanti had grinned and swept her into his arms.

"Both," he'd agreed, kissing her hungrily.

Now Natalie could feel that jungle air simmering between them.

Christo paused at the door, pushing it open for her, then stepping aside to let her enter. But he didn't move back, made no move to leave her there.

She turned and paused, looking up at him. He stood so close she could see the lines of the thread in the black tux jacket he wore. She remembered the smoothness of it under her fingers when they'd danced. Remembered what it had been like to have his arms around her tonight, the pulse of his body in time with hers. Remembered the fire in his hooded eyes as he'd looked at her.

Felt even now the electricity that seemed to sing in her blood.

A look up at Christo's face told her he was remembering it and feeling it, too. His gaze was still hot and dark and hungry. A muscle seemed to tick in his jaw.

Would he?

Should they?

It wasn't hers to say. She knew that. This was his home, his family, his charade.

And if they did, what would it do to her? Did she want to find out? When he didn't speak, just stood there, she knew she had to say something.

"It was a lovely wedding. A beautiful day." She wished her voice wouldn't waver.

"Yes." Christo nodded. He didn't blink. And his gaze never left hers.

She remembered that gaze. It had fastened on her the night he had finally taken her to his bed. It had mesmerized her, devoured her. And tonight it was doing exactly the same.

She should look away. Step back. Close the door. Lock it.

Instead she stood there, a doe trapped in headlights. "Christo." His name on her lips was barely more than a whisper. She paused and ran her tongue over them. The very air seemed to shimmer between them.

"Send me away." His voice was harsh.

She frowned at the tone. "What?"

His jaw tightened. "You heard me, Nat. Tell me to go."

She hesitated, then drew a breath, steadying herself. She knew what he was demanding. And she knew the wisdom of it. But she couldn't do it.

Fool that she was, she could not turn her back on him. He was the one who insisted that there was nothing between them. He was the one who had said, "I want you." Let him be the one to walk away.

So she looked up and met his gaze steadily. "Why?"

He blinked, as if her response startled him. "You know why," he said roughly.

She put a hand on the fine tropical wool of his coat. "Because you want me to be your conscience."

"Because I want you to protect yourself!"

"And if I don't want to be protected?" She lifted her gaze, raised her brows, challenged him.

He sucked in a harsh breath. "*Por Deus!* For God's sake, Natalic!"

She dropped her hand and shrugged with as much lightness as she could manage. "What if I don't?" she persisted.

"I don't do love," he reminded her harshly. "I don't do marriage."

It hurt to hear the words, spelling it out again. But she simply nodded. "I know that," she said evenly. "You aren't telling me anything new, Christo. I knew that before I came down here with you. That's why you asked me, isn't it? Because I knew and I could still come along and be 'believable'?"

His gaze became almost a glare now, but she didn't turn away. It was true. She knew it and he knew it.

"Send me away, Nat," he said again.

And once more, slowly but deliberately, she shook her head. "No."

Then she backed into her small cottage, but left the door open, watching him, her eyes never leaving his.

Seconds passed. Three. Five. Maybe even ten. She didn't count. She could see the struggle on his face. And then the resignation.

"Fine, damn it," he said at last. "If this is what you want—" And he strode in after her. He looked almost menacing, but she didn't back down.

"Is it what you want, Christo?" she asked him quietly.

"You know it is." He was unfastening his bow tie and jerking it loose, trying to shrug off his jacket and pulling at the buttons of his shirt even as he spoke.

Natalie pushed the door closed behind him. Then she shut her eyes in a fervent prayer that, however painful it would be when Christo left her and went his own way, the memory of this night would be enough. That having it, cherishing it, hanging on to it forever, would sustain her forever. Maybe she was a fool. Maybe she was making the biggest mistake of her life.

Or maybe she'd already made that when she'd fallen in love with him—and this was the best she could get.

Whichever…she turned and touched him, stilled his hands with hers. Then she swallowed and looked up to smile at him. "Let me."

He wanted to refuse. She could see it on his face. Christo Savas was not a patient man. Natalie knew he would have happily ripped his shirt right off, then started on her dress. And he could have undressed them both in a few seconds flat.

But she didn't want that.

If tonight was going to last her a lifetime, she was determined to make the most of it. She would love him, share her bed with him, give and take pleasure—but she wanted it deliberate—and she wanted it slow.

"Nat," he said raggedly.

But she shook her head. "Let me," she whispered again. And slowly and carefully she undid the buttons of his dress shirt while he stood before her, his teeth clenched, his breathing quick and shallow.

When she had them undone, he raised his hands to take the shirt off, but she stayed them again. "Please."

His breath hissed through his teeth. "You're going to kill me," he said.

She smiled. "I hope not." She slanted a glance at him. "If you're worried, I could send you away," she reminded him.

"Then," he muttered. "Not now."

Now they had passed the point of no return. Natalie ran her hands down first one of his arms, and then the other, carefully removing his cufflinks. While he simmered with impatience, she tugged his shirttails out of his black trousers. Then and only then did she push the shirt back off his shoulders and peel it away from his body.

He yanked off his undershirt before she could take a breath.

"Christo!"

"I'm on fire for you."

"The feeling is mutual," she told him truthfully. "But we have all night."

He shook his head as he toed off first one shoe and then the other, then kicked them aside. His hands went to his belt.

"Mine," Natalie said firmly and got there before him.

He made a sound of impatience, but he stood still and let her unfasten the belt, then open it. Then, with her gaze meeting his, she slid down the zip of his trousers. A muscle in his jaw ticked, and she trailed her fingers over his straining erection and heard him grind his teeth.

"I want your dress off," he told her. His voice was thick and rough. "Now."

Natalie nodded and turned her back to him so he could undo the buttons. She hadn't chosen this dress to be a challenge. But it was. No zipper slid down the length of its silken back. Instead, there was a row of tiny fabric-covered buttons. Alondra, one of Katia's cousins, had done them all up for her this afternoon.

"Oh, Christo is going to kill you," she'd giggled.

Natalie had doubted it. Christo had been determinedly hands-off during the whole trip. Not now. Now she heard the harsh exhalation of his breath as his trembling hands fumbled with the buttons.

"You did this deliberately." Exasperation mingled with amusement in his tone.

Natalie turned her head to look at him. "I didn't. Really," she protested.

"It's been driving me nuts all day. Provocative as hell."

"It's very modest," she said. It was, too. A sleeveless dress, yes, but with a high neckline, the emerald silk covered all essentials very thoroughly.

"It fits you like a glove. Every man out there was ogling your curves."

"Every man out there was looking at Katia."

"I wasn't."

He sucked in another breath as he continued to battle the buttons. "And that slit you have on the side!" He groaned.

"So I can walk," she said. "The dress is cut very narrowly."

"Damned right it is. And then you dance and show a glimpse of that leg. And then—it's gone again!"

"Nice to know it had an effect," she murmured.

His laugh was ragged. "Oh, it had an effect." His fingers stilled against her back. "You didn't really like this dress all that well anyway, did you?" And before she could reply, he tore it the rest of the way down the back.

"Christo!"

He didn't answer, just pushed it off her shoulders letting it pool at her feet. His fingers skimmed down the half slip she wore and then he unfastened her bra and took it off, too. "Better," he muttered. "Much better."

She only wore a pair of brief panties now, and when he turned her in his arms and held her so he could look at her, his hooded eyes were dark with desire.

Instinctively, Natalie wanted to cover herself. But Christo held her wrists in his hands as he stood and stared at her. And his gaze was so rapt that Natalie could do no more than stare back. She watched the quick rise and fall of his chest and the convulsive working of his Adam's apple.

"You are so beautiful." He breathed the words as he loosed her wrists and ran trembling fingers up the length of her arms to her shoulders. His fingers slid through her hair, then ran lightly down her back to hook in the waistband of her panties and draw them down.

Silently she stepped out of them and, naked to his gaze, reached out to do the same to him. He started to do it himself, but the light touch of her hands stopped him and he stood and let her have her way. And then he was as naked as she, and she could only stare, then let her fingers slide lightly down his chest and belly, along the length of his shaft, watching his whole body tense under her touch.

She reached beneath to cup him in her hands, to hold

him, and he shifted and let out a shaky breath. "Nat," his voice sounded strangled. "You're going to burn me down."

She looked up at him, then lowered her lids, smiled and leaned in to press a kiss to his lips. "Am I?"

"Yes! Oh, yes." The words hissed between his teeth and then he moved. In barely an instant he had borne her back on the bed, rolling her beneath him and sliding between her legs.

She would have liked it to last longer, wanted more to savor. But she knew she had pushed him making him wait this long, insisting on having her way. And so she opened to him, smiled up at him—and was surprised when, instead of joining his body with hers, he rolled off so that he lay beside her.

"What?" She lifted her head to look at him.

It was his turn to smile, albeit wryly. "I've decided you're right," he said, his voice still rough and edgy with desire. "Why hurry?" He ran a hand down her side, making her sensitive nerve endings shiver delightedly. "We've got all night."

At her obvious surprise, Christo just laughed, then leaned across to kiss her. "Don't we?" he murmured against her lips. She loved the warmth of his mouth on hers, the light touch of his tongue, the teasing nibble of his teeth.

"All night," Natalie agreed.

And she refused to let herself think beyond it.

He shouldn't be here. Shouldn't have given in to temptation. But somehow, where Natalie was concerned, Christo had no will to resist.

What man in possession of all the right hormones could have spent the day with her, have held her hand, pressed his against the small of her back, danced with her, caught the occasional glimpse of the tanned length of her leg whenever her dress split halfway to the top of her thigh, saw her drink from his glass at exactly the same spot he had, and felt the warm invitation of her lips when he'd swept her close at the end of that last dance, and then take her to her door and walk away?

If she'd sent him…if she'd shaken her head and said no…he would have done it. He knew that. He wouldn't do what she didn't want him to.

But she hadn't said no.

So how could he?

He wanted her too badly. Had been like a dying man in the desert this whole week—every glimpse of Natalie an oasis promising to slake his desire—and all week long he'd deliberately turned away.

And tonight he couldn't. He knew he would never have slept a wink all night if he'd gone to his own room. An icy shower or a mile-long swim would have done nothing to quell the aching need within him.

He'd pay for it later. Whatever it was, he would pay the price.

But tonight—just this night—he had to spend with Natalie.

He had to touch her, taste her, watch her face as he stroked her skin and kissed her lips and, ultimately, buried himself inside her. But the very thoughts that made the aching need grow, also made him want to make it last. She'd been right—there was no need to rush.

And so he backed off. To take it slowly. To savor her. Love her.

He reined in all his urgent instincts and set about doing just that. He kissed his way across her shoulder and down her arm. He nibbled her fingers. And when she shivered and would have balled them into a fist, he nosed them open again and pressed kisses on the palm of her hand. First one, then the other.

And when he let go of them, he felt them clench in his hair as he nuzzled her belly and moved south toward the juncture of her thighs.

"Christo!" It was somewhere between a laugh, a gasp and a protest.

"Shh." He breathed on her curls, parted her, stroked her, felt her body tremble. Her fingers tightened in his scalp. She tugged on his hair.

He smiled. Her toes curled.

"Christo!" And he was glad he'd had a haircut as she gave a hard yank and pulled him up on top of her.

"You don't like that?"

"Mm, well." She shifted. "I don't mind, but—"

"You don't mind?" He grinned.

"All right, yes. It's—lovely. It makes me crazy. I want—" But she stopped and shook her head.

"You want?" he pressed.

She wrapped her legs around him. "I want you."

There was no doubt he wanted her just as much. No way to deny it. And no way to hold back now. He was too close to coming. Too close to making himself a part of her. Impossible, however much he might want to, to pull away again.

He shifted, but she held him fast.

"You're not—" she said.

"—going anywhere," he promised. "Only here," he added as she released her grip enough so that he could settle in and fill her. His eyes squeezed shut at the slick sweet heat that surrounded him. He held perfectly still, drew a steadying breath, knew that if he moved just once it would be all over.

And then her fingers walked down his back, her back arched and she lifted to draw him even further in. Christo groaned, felt the urgency build despite himself, and knew again that the temptation of Natalie Ross was beyond his will power to resist.

She had him.

He lost himself, shattering at the same time he rejoiced as he felt the ripple and shudder of Natalie's climax around him.

Natalie didn't sleep.

There was no time. She needed every moment in his embrace to store up memories that would have to last her a lifetime. She nuzzled her nose against the crisp softness of his hair. She trailed her fingers lightly along the rough stubble of his jaw. And she smiled at the half-moons of incredibly long dark lashes that Christo had no idea were so sexy.

He was funny that way. When she'd first met him, she'd been dazzled by his drop-dead good looks, his strong bones, his engaging grin, and those thick dark lashes that he often regarded you from beneath, making you wonder what he was thinking.

It was, one of the office girls once said, a male version of the come-hither look. And certainly every unattached woman at the firm would have followed him wherever he asked.

A goodly number of his women clients—even ones determined to swear off men after their divorces—would do the same. Natalie had seen it in their faces.

Christo was unaware of it. He didn't flirt. Not intentionally, at least. He was comfortable in his skin, but he didn't use his looks to manipulate. He didn't deliberately enchant. It was purely unintentional, and all the more effective for being so.

He was such a good man. Such a strong man. Such a kind man. She'd had inklings of it three years ago. She'd seen him in action at work and with Jamii—and now just this past week.

He'd given of himself so much this week.

For a man who didn't do family, he had put himself out day after day. He'd made the arrangements his father couldn't be bothered to make. He'd been there, stable and steady and caring, when she knew he didn't want to be here at all.

Except for his grandmother.

He loved her.

Natalie did, too, now. And felt almighty guilty for deceiving her. She would live with that guilt the rest of her life, no doubt. Part of the penalty for loving where her heart should not have loved.

She burrowed closer to him, as if she might be able simply to absorb him into her being the way she held him in her heart. He sighed and, still sleeping, wrapped her more tightly in his embrace.

Yes, Natalie thought. *Oh, yes. Please.*

But she knew it was only for the moment. Not even the whole night.

He would wake and he would leave her alone here, just as he had every other time they'd shared a bed. She tried not to move, tried to hang on as long as she could.

But then he sighed and shifted. His eyes opened and met hers in the moonlit night. His face was grave. There was no smile now. No wry humor. And Natalie expected the misery to begin now.

He leaned in to close the distance between their lips. His warm mouth touched hers, lingered and then slowly pulled away. And Natalie steeled herself not to cling. In fact, she even deliberately rolled away before he did.

She was shocked when she didn't feel the mattress shift as Christo left the bed. He didn't leave. Instead he moved closer, spooned himself around her and drew her back against his chest.

Her body tensed with surprise. Then she held her breath and waited for him to pull away again. His breath was warm on the nape of her neck. It stirred the tendrils of her hair. He shifted. Settled.

"Christo?" She barely breathed his name.

"Mmm." It wasn't an answer so much as a sigh. Of contentment?

She didn't dare hope. All she did was clutch his fingers in hers against her breasts and hang on as if she could hold him there forever.

She couldn't, of course. She knew that. It was pretence. It was undoubtedly folly. But it was all she had.

And when the tears leaked from the corners of her eyes and slid down to dampen the pillow, she made certain he never knew.

His grandmother was waiting when he came to the house the next morning. She made coffee and put a cup in front of him wordlessly, then sat down at the table opposite before she spoke.

What she said did not make the morning any easier.

"It is good, Christo." She had one of her grave gentle smiles on her face. "You and Natalie are good."

Good liars, he thought grimly. But they were almost out of it now. Their plane left early this evening. The charade would be over soon.

He would have liked to turn and take his coffee out on the deck, but he knew he was expected to stay. So he sat where he was and tried not to fidget, though he felt the way he used to when he'd done something wrong— broken a window, sassed the gardener—and was afraid she'd find out.

Avó nodded now and regarded him over the top of her coffee cup. "You have chosen well." Her gaze rested on him with deep love. Then she added with a nod of approval, "I knew you would."

Which effectively made him feel even worse. She liked Natalie—which he'd known she would—and he was taking advantage of how well he knew her to pull the wool over her eyes.

He forced a smile. "I'm glad you approve."

She reached across the table to touch his hand. "I do."

Her touch was dry and warm, and her fingers seemed to tremble a bit. He thought she looked frail this morning, as if the wedding had taken everything out of her, as if she'd been holding herself together for it, and now that it was past, she could let go.

Don't let go, he wanted to beg her. *You can't.* He couldn't imagine a world without her calm steadying presence. His throat felt thick and tight. He swallowed hard.

"Your father will be happy, I think," she said with a faint smile and he knew she was comparing Xanti's choice to his own. "But they will throw things."

Christo's mouth curved at one corner. "You think?"

Avó nodded. "Oh, *sim.* Katia? She will be a challenge for Xanti. Like your mother was."

Christo's brows lifted. He didn't know his grandmother had ever even met his mother. She'd never talked about her.

She smiled again, but it was a sad, wry smile. "They were a pair, Xanti and Aurora. Mad and young and far too stubborn for their own good. They each wanted the other—and their lives so different—and neither would give an inch."

Christo stared at her, then shook his head. "I didn't know. I thought they—"

But he didn't want to say what he'd thought. He'd always assumed they had been barely more than ships passing in the night. Each of them a one-night stand for the other until Xanti had come back.

Now he steepled his fingers. "No one ever said."

Avó lifted bony shoulders. "They argued. They battled. They slammed doors. And in the end Aurora stamped out. Went home to America. She didn't tell him about you. When he went to see her, it was a shock to find you. And of course, he must marry her because that is the sort of man Xanti is."

"Impractical," Christo said.

"Idealistic. Stubborn. And your mother the same. They married. But neither would change. Not then." She spread her hands. "People are who they are."

"Yes." He could agree with that.

"They must make their own decisions. Be true to themselves."

"Yes."

"But not shortchange themselves. It is good that Xanti has finally realized this."

"Yes."

Her gaze dropped and she contemplated her coffee cup for a long moment, then she lifted it again and met his. "I am happy for him. Happy to go seeing him happy."

"You're not going anywhere," Christo protested.

"I am," Avó told him. "I am old. I am sick. I am ready."

"I'm not!"

She laughed softly. "Things are not always the way we want them to be. You have given me great joy, Christo. You have made my life so much better. When Xanti told me about you, he thought I would be angry, that I would not want to see this child he had made. I was angry that he would not be a better father. But never with you, Christo *meu*. Things might not have been the way I wanted them, but they were good. And you only brought happiness when you came."

"I didn't come often enough," he told her urgently. He had hold of her hand now, was turning it over in his, chaffing it between his fingers as if he could rub more life—more years—into her. "I'll stay."

She shook her head. "No. You have a life to go back to. You came now, when it was important."

"For Xanti! I'll stay for you."

"Go home," Avó said firmly. She lifted his fingers to her lips and kissed them. "You will take me with you in your heart."

He had been gone when she woke up, of course.

Natalie knew he would be. She let her mind reflect on the memories she had made and, thank God, they were vivid. She went through the motions of packing and, at the same time, trying to make more memories of the house, of the garden, of the way the winter sun slanted through the blinds. She picked up the pillow on which Christo had lain his head and she pressed it to her face to draw in his scent. To keep it and hold it. To hang onto every tiny morsel of this moment.

She could see him on the deck across the garden. He was

helping his grandmother into a chair and settling her in. There was such gentleness in him. She remembered him with Toby in the office, how strong, how supportive. She remembered him with Jamii in the ocean, how protective, how careful with her, at the same time he'd urged her to believe in her own abilities. He gave and he gave.

And he would take nothing for himself.

Because he didn't want anything, she reminded herself.

No, not quite true. He'd wanted her last night. Sex he would take. It was love and commitment he didn't trust.

"Oh, Christo," she murmured aloud, hugging his pillow against her breasts, rocking back and forth, tears springing to her eyes again. But he wouldn't want her crying over him.

"Be tough," he'd told Jamii. "Do what you need to do."

And Jamii had. And so would she.

But it was hard.

And she could only bow her head when, as they were leaving, while Christo was putting the suitcases in the trunk of a rental car, Avó took her hand urgently.

"You love my Christo," she said, her dark eyes glittering with strong emotion. It was an affirmation, not a question.

Natalie was glad because she couldn't have lied, and Christo would have heard the truth in her voice if she'd had to answer. She smiled and squeezed his grandmother's fingers lightly.

But Avó wasn't done.

"You love him forever." His grandmother's tone was urgent now, and this time her words weren't a statement so much as a command. Her fingers crushed Natalie's. Their gazes met, clung.

Promise me, the old woman's eyes seemed to demand.

And Natalie nodded numbly. *I will,* she said the words in her heart.

It was nothing but the truth.

CHAPTER TEN

HARD work, Natalie's grandfather used to say, cured all ills.

"What about stubbed toes?" she'd asked him doubtfully. "What about migraines?"

"Ah well, you'll see," he had said, smiling at her over the top of his trifocals with the wisdom of his eighty years.

And now she did.

Stubbed toes were nothing. Even migraines didn't hurt like this did. She was alone. Christo didn't call. Christo didn't come by. To Christo, no doubt, she had ceased to exist.

And so she threw herself into her work. She got up at five—what point was there to staying in bed when she almost never slept?—and she did all the bookkeeping and invoicing and paperwork that needed to be done before Sophy ever appeared at the office.

"It's the time change," she explained before Sophy could even ask.

"It's *two* hours," Sophy said archly.

Natalie shrugged irritably. "I can't help it. I'm awake."

"Apparently. But it isn't the time change keeping you up," Sophy said with a look that defied her to dispute it.

As she couldn't, Natalie focused determinedly on the computer screen.

"Have you heard from him?"

Natalie debated pretending that she had no idea what Sophy was driving at and deliberately didn't look up. But even as she stared at the screen, she knew there was no point in denying it.

"I haven't," she said, trying to keep her tone even. "I don't expect to."

She could feel Sophy's gaze so intent on her that it was almost like a physical touch. But she didn't lift her eyes to meet it. There was a long silence, and then Sophy said quietly, "Maybe you will."

There was an even longer silence before Natalie replied. "Maybe."

But she wasn't holding out hope.

"I've come to bring you some peaches," Laura said, setting a mammoth bag on the countertop in Natalie's kitchen.

It was an unannounced visit—and one that Natalie was sure owed only part of its purpose to the unloading of excess fruit from the tree in the small garden. It had been ten days since she'd returned from Brazil, and she hadn't seen her mother yet.

She'd spoken with her, of course. She'd rung her the night they'd got back, and Laura had been all curiosity and eager speculative questions—questions which Natalie knew she couldn't answer, didn't want to try.

She could not have lied any more by that time if her life had depended on it.

"We'll talk later," she'd promised her mother. "I'm really tired."

She'd been playing the "tired" card and the "heavy

work load" card ever since. And clearly Laura's patience had worn thin.

"Christo said you had a lovely time in Brazil," her mother reported, bright eyes sparkling as she watched Natalie chop vegetables for the stir fry she was making. The subtext, Natalie had no trouble understanding was *You, on the other hand, haven't told me a thing.*

"We did," she said. There was a God, she decided, because it was an onion she was chopping and the tears already streaming down her face made the conversation a whole lot easier.

"Not that you've told me anything about it," Laura added with a slightly indignant huff.

"I've been busy. I left Sophy to do everything for a week. I need to put in my time now. Besides, you've obviously talked to Christo."

Her mother made a despairing sound. "He's a man. Men don't talk."

Or if they did, they didn't say the words you wanted to hear, Natalie thought. She concentrated on the onion.

"He says the wedding went very well." Laura added. It was too much to hope that she would leave the peaches and go without an attempt at the third degree. Indeed, even as Natalie thought it, her mother reached around her and put on the kettle for tea. "And his grandmother liked you."

"Yes." Chop, chop.

Laura took down two mugs from the cupboard and added a tea bag to each. "I was so surprised he did that. And then I…well, I hoped…" her mother added, giving her a speculative look.

"Don't," Natalie said firmly. "You know it was business. A favor. Of sorts. Actually, I'm surprised you approved."

"Of the subterfuge, you mean? It wasn't my place to approve or disapprove," Laura said, surprising her. "I've learned over the years not to expect things will always be the way I want them to be."

Natalie nodded. She was learning that, too.

"Was it…all right then?" her mother asked gently.

Natalie swallowed. She didn't want understanding right now. She was too close to the edge. She didn't need sympathy, either. Didn't want her mother to notice how her hands were suddenly shaking.

"It was fine," she said softly.

There was a long silence, and she wondered if her mother would challenge her. But she didn't. She settled into one of the kitchen chairs and said, "What was the best part?"

Natalie wondered if it might be a tactic—an oblique probe. Get her daughter to talk, then lead the discussion where she wanted it to go. Or maybe it was just small talk to ease the situation. Her mother could do that, too.

And so could she. "The flowers," Natalie said.

"Flowers?"

"So many. So colorful. So different from what we're used to." Natalie dumped the chopped onion onto the plate with the other vegetables, then turned to give her mother a bright smile.

Laura looked surprised, but only a bit doubtful. "I'd like to see them sometime."

"Maybe next time there's a family wedding Christo will take you," Natalie said with all the cheer she could muster.

Laura shook her head. "I don't think it will be a wedding he'll be going back for."

At her mother's tone, Natalie stopped and looked up. "What do you mean?" she said with a hard cold lump of something dreadful settling in her stomach.

Laura sighed. "His grandmother has been very ill."

Natalie wanted to protest. But the words caught in her throat. She took a careful breath. "I know. She was ill when we were there. But she didn't want to admit it. She's worse?"

"Yes."

Natalie was sure that his grandmother's illness had been the reason Christo had been so remote and silent on the plane all the way home. He'd barely said a dozen words the whole trip. She had wanted to comfort him. To say something to make him feel better. But there was nothing to say, nothing that would help.

The only thing she'd dared to do was reach for his hand on the armrest, curve her fingers around his and hold on.

She half expected he'd give her a quick squeeze and deliberately let go. But instead he had turned his hand over and wrapped his fingers around hers. They'd tightened in a gentle squeeze, but when the pressure eased, he didn't let go.

He didn't speak, though. For nearly the entire journey he had stared out the window, silent as a stone.

Only when they'd arrived back at her house did he say more than three words at a time. Then he'd said gravely, almost formally, "Thank you, Natalie. I couldn't have done it without you."

She'd been tempted to say something flippant in the face of his distant formality. Something like, *Damned right you couldn't. Hard to pretend you have a fiancée when you can't produce her.*

But that would have been pointless. It would have betrayed how much his leaving her was going to hurt. It would have told him that her determinedly casual acceptance of a mere affair was a lie.

She'd had enough of lies. But she'd needed that last one

to make the break. And so she'd merely nodded and said quietly, "I was glad to do it."

She would carry those memories with her for the rest of her days. She would take them out and remember them—remember him—always.

He never said, "I'll see you again."

He never said, "I'll call you."

He never even said, "I'd like to go to bed with you again."

So maybe he already knew she'd broken the rules.

He'd held out his hand to her in farewell. It had all been very polite. Proper. The appropriate end to a business arrangement, she supposed.

They'd managed faint smiles, though they had barely even looked at each other. For one fleeting moment their gazes had connected and quickly he'd said, "Good-bye," and dropped her hand.

And then with another "Thank you again," he'd turned abruptly and walked away.

Since then Natalie hadn't heard a word. Didn't expect to. Knew she never would.

She hadn't talked about him, either. Couldn't.

But apparently avoidance could only be counted on to work for a short time. So Natalie steeled herself to get through it.

"I liked his grandmother a lot," she said.

Laura nodded. "Christo certainly thinks the world of her."

"Is he going back to Brazil?"

"I expect so." Laura looked sad. The kettle whistled and she got up to pour the water for tea. "He's away right now. I told him he should take a little vacation. He's been very distracted since he got back. That's not like Christo."

"No."

Had he gone on his "little vacation" alone? Or had he

already found a woman to replace her in his bed? The knife wobbled in her hand and she nearly sliced her fingers.

"I thought at first it was your fault." Laura's words jerked her back to the moment.

"My fault? What was my fault?"

"His distraction. I thought you might have done something to upset him."

"No," Natalie said firmly. "Except where his grandmother is concerned, Christo doesn't do upset." She knew that all too well.

Her mother nodded. "Yes. When he told me how ill she was, I realized what was really bothering him."

"Nothing to do with me." Natalie swallowed against the lump in her throat. It shouldn't hurt. It was selfish even to wish she'd mattered a little. She whacked the celery into little bits and dumped them into the wok.

"I took pictures at the wedding," she told her mother. "Would you like to see them?"

Laura brightened. "That would be lovely."

It wouldn't. It would hurt right down to the bone. But looking at them and forcing herself to talk casually and rationally about the time she'd spent in Brazil—with Christo—would be salutary.

"Have some dinner with me and I'll show them to you after."

Laura beamed at her. Natalie did her best to smile back. She made a real effort that evening to act like a sane, sensible, grown-up woman, a heart-whole woman. And she managed—more or less.

She didn't burst into tears. She didn't choke up—much. When her voice wobbled once or twice, Laura put it down to her concern about Christo's grandmother and the emotions evoked by a beautiful wedding.

Natalie certainly didn't disagree with her.

And after Laura left, she congratulated herself on a performance well done. She would get over him. She would cope without him.

And if she cried herself to sleep that night, she told herself firmly that things would get better. They had to.

She couldn't spend the next sixty years doing this.

The rain was coming down in buckets. It was miserable. Cold. Those who thought southern California couldn't get cold should be here now, Natalie thought, shivering as she stared out at the bleak September morning. The chill went right to the bone.

"I can't remember when it ever rained in September," she said to Sophy when her cousin called.

"Last year," Sophy said briskly. "What's wrong with you?"

"Nothing."

Everything. Still. Maybe it wasn't the chill of the weather. Maybe it was deep inside. It had been almost a month since she'd come home, and she could honestly say that the day of Christo's father's wedding under the winter sun of Brazil was the last time she'd been warm.

Now, as she stared out the window of her apartment at the water streaming down the pane, she thought that at least it suited her mood.

If it hadn't been nearly noon, she'd have used the excuse of it being Saturday and gone back to bed and pulled the covers over her head.

As it was, she'd been sitting in a huddled lump on her sofa wishing she had Herbie, at least, to cuddle. She felt bereft. Lost. Alone. She almost hadn't answered the phone when Sophy rang. But she had to stop behaving like a slug.

"I'm fine," she said with all the firmness she could

manage when Sophy's silence made it clear her cousin doubted that.

"Yeah, right," Sophy said. "You need to get out. Do something! I've been patient, waiting for you to snap out of it."

"I'm snapping," Natalie muttered. "It's just taking a while."

"Like a saggy rubber band," Sophy retorted. "Honestly. You're pathetic. I didn't sit home after George and I broke up."

"It's not the same thing."

"Of course it is. How long are you going to lie to yourself?"

"I'm not lying to myself!"

"Much," Sophy snorted. "You're dragging around, moping about him."

No doubt which "him" she meant. And Natalie knew better than to deny it. "It's not the same. I wasn't married to Christo. I went to Brazil with him. If I lied to anyone, I lied to his grandmother. By implication if not in fact. And I'm not proud of it."

"I suppose not," Sophy said, a surprising note of gentle commiseration in her voice now. "How is she?"

"I don't know."

Even her mother had had no news. Or if she had, she hadn't passed it on to Natalie. It had been two weeks since she'd shared dinner and photographs with her mother. They'd chatted briefly on the phone since. But since Christo was still gone, Laura had gone back to Iowa for a visit.

"I'm sorry," Sophy said. "But really, Nat, you have to get past it. You're twenty-five years old. You have a long life ahead of you. There will be other men. Better men," Sophy added firmly.

Natalie wished she could believe that. "Yeah," she said dully. "I'm sure you're right."

"I am right. The Savas men are pains in the butt. I speak from experience," she added drily.

"Yes." Natalie wished she believed that, too. But she didn't.

It was her own idiocy that had brought her to this. Christo had never meant to hurt her. He never would have asked her to go with him if he hadn't trusted her word that her heart wasn't involved.

I don't do love. I don't do marriage. He couldn't have been more explicit.

So if she was hurting now, it was her own fault, not his. He'd warned her.

She was the one who'd thought she would be safe.

Or, if not safe—because she wasn't that self-deluded—at least she'd promised herself that the joy she would know during those few brief days with him at his father's wedding would be worth the pain she'd feel afterwards.

The more fool she.

"It's my fault," she told Sophy now.

Sophy made a rude noise. "Which is exactly what I think of that," she said tartly in case Natalie needed it spelled out. "You need to go out. I'll find you a date."

"No."

"I will," Sophy vowed. "A good man."

"Don't you dare."

"Wait right there." Sophy was getting into it now. "I'll send him over."

"Sophy," Natalie warned her.

"What else are you doing this dreary morning?"

"I could have gone to Disneyland with Dan and Co."

"But you didn't," Sophy pointed out.

"Because it's raining."

"Because you're sopping around feeling sorry for yourself. You need waking up. Jolting. I've got just the thing. A husband-for-hire."

"No!"

"Come on, Nat. We have a new guy on the books. Remember cousin Walter's friend Larry?"

"I said, no!" Unable even to joke about it, Natalie hung up.

She went into the kitchen and put on the kettle to make herself a cup of tea. *Get a grip,* she told herself. *Sophy cares. She's only kidding.* The kettle had barely whistled when there was a sharp knock on her front door.

"Oh, no."

Because Sophy had taken the joke one step too far. Was Walter's friend Larry that desperate for a bit of work that he'd agreed to come out on a rainy Saturday just to help Sophy annoy her cousin?

Well, too bad. It wasn't funny, and Natalie was sorry that she was going to bite some poor guy's head off, but really—

There was a second sharp knock on the door.

She had barely pasted on her polite, I'm-the-boss smile before she jerked open the door. "Look, I don't care what Sophy told you, I do not need—"

It wasn't cousin Walter's friend Larry.

Natalie's words dried up. She could only stare.

Christo stared back. And there was such a look of hunger and anguish in his bleak shadowed eyes that she'd never seen anything like it before. Not even the last night in Brazil when he'd made love with her.

She stood stock-still, her mouth open, but no sound came out. At last she croaked, "What do you want?"

"To marry you. Will you?"

It was the last thing she expected to hear.

She couldn't have heard him right. It had to be wishful thinking, self-delusion. Maybe she had even imagined him as well. She blinked furiously, expecting Christo to be a mirage, certain that cousin Walter's friend Larry would materialize in his stead.

"Nat?" he said impatiently. It was Christo's gruff voice that had her eyes snapping open again to see him still standing there.

"What?"

"I'm getting soaked." He was agitated, annoyed, edgy as hell—and very definitely real.

"Oh! Er—right. Come in." She yanked the door open wider, and Christo came in to drip on the carpet. He pulled off his jacket, and Natalie took it from him with nerveless fingers, then carried it to the kitchen to hang over the back of a chair, taking refuge in the mundane because her mind was reeling. When she came back he was standing right where she'd left him.

"I'll get you a towel," she said.

He shook his head, his eyes boring into hers. "Never mind the towel. Just answer the question." His voice held none of the indifference she was so used to hearing. He sounded edgy and decidedly tense.

Once more their gazes met. And she wondered if she had really heard him right, after all. She might have missed him. Not been here at all. Could easily have gone to Disneyland with Dan, Kelly and Jamii.

Neither the rain nor her "acting soppy," in Sophy's words, had been the real reason she hadn't gone. The real reason was that she hadn't wanted to face Jamii. Her mother and Sophy might be put off by rebuffs or deflections, but Jamii wouldn't have been. She would have wanted to know all about her trip, all about Christo—where they'd gone, what they'd done. She wouldn't have been deflected.

And Natalie couldn't have talked about him without

her voice breaking. Not without tears she had no business shedding sliding down her cheeks—because she
fully expected she wouldn't see him again. Not in any
way that mattered.

And now here he was, in her living room, tense and
edgy, staring at her. "Will you marry me?"

"You don't do marriage," she reminded him.

He ran his tongue over his lips, then dipped his head in
acknowledgment. "I thought I didn't."

"And now you do?" She couldn't make it a statement.
She had too many doubts.

"Yes."

"Just like that?"

"Yes." His answer was firm and steady, and Natalie
found herself burning under the intensity of his gaze.

But she needed to know more. Lots more.

"Why?"

"Because I love you."

She hadn't expected that. She had expected some
rational sensible argument. A logical lawyerly exposition.
Not stark words that cut right to the depths of her soul.
Words she desperately wanted to believe. And didn't.
Couldn't. Not yet.

"You don't do love, either."

He grimaced. "I said a lot of stupid things. Thought a
lot of stupid things. And it's true, I didn't *want* to fall in
love. I didn't want to mess up my life!"

"Thank you very much," Natalie said drily past the lump
in her throat.

He raked a hand through damp spiky hair, then began
to pace around the room. "I didn't mean that. I meant…I
didn't believe in commitment. The 'til-death-do-us-part
stuff. I never saw it work." The look he gave her was an-

guished. "Why buy into that? It seemed like too much of a risk."

"And now it doesn't?"

He stopped and faced her squarely. "Now I don't have any choice."

"Of course you have a choice," she said with all the coldness she could muster. "No one's holding a gun to your head. You can walk right back out that door this minute."

"I don't want—"

But she pressed on, making herself say it. "I knew what the score was, Christo. I took your terms. And I'm not pining away." She wouldn't, damn it. Even if it felt as if she would. She looked him in the eyes. "I never begged you to come."

His mouth twisted wryly. "No," he admitted. "I'm the one on my knees."

And the look he gave her very nearly melted her where she stood. But she held fast, didn't move.

"I love you, Nat. I didn't want to! God help me, I didn't want to care. It's a hell of a risk. Ask any of my clients. Ask your own mother!" He started pacing again, making the room shrink even further. "I thought I never would. Thought if I just drew boundaries, I'd be safe." He turned and looked back at her, a hard glitter in his dark jade eyes. "There is no safety where you're concerned. You get past all my boundaries, Nat. You break down all my walls. You're with me every step all day long. Wherever I am, you're there!"

Natalie didn't know if it was an accusation or a declaration of love. He looked miserable.

She shrugged. "Sorry."

"Don't be sorry." His voice was ragged. "I've never been happier in my life."

She almost laughed at that. "Right. Of course you are. You look like you're jumping for joy."

"Not now, damn it. Then! When we were together. At the beach. In Brazil. At work. At home. Whenever I'm with you. Whenever you're with me. Not just in bed, Nat," he added. "Though I'll admit that's part of it."

Natalie found herself reaching for the back of the armchair closest to her. She needed to hang onto it. Needed the support. The way the revelations were coming she thought she might fall right down.

"What I feel scares the hell out of me," he told her frankly. "How could it not? I've seen so many couples who are screwed up. So many marriages, so many relationships—my own parents above all—go wrong." He drew a breath. "But not to try—" He shook his head. "To give up the best thing that ever happened to me without even asking you to try with me—I can't do that."

He stopped speaking. Outside the rain pounded down. In here there was only the pounding of their hearts, so loud Natalie thought she could even hear them, then realized it was the blood hammering through her veins.

Consciously, deliberately, she loosed her grip on the back of the chair, took a breath, formed her thoughts, started to speak, but Christo wasn't finished.

"I know your father hurt you when he left your mother. I know what he did made you wary of marriage. And I know you said you don't want to get married. I have no right to ask you. It's changing the rules. It's not playing fair. It's—"

"Love."

Christo stopped. Stared at her. "What?"

Natalie ventured a tremulous smile. "It's love," she repeated, her voice stronger now, more confident. "I understand about love, Christo. I love you." She said the words slowly, deliberately, infusing them with every bit of the intensity she was feeling.

For a long moment Christo didn't move. Didn't speak. It was as if he didn't believe his ears—or her words.

And then, when she didn't say anything else, when she just stood there, looking at him with her heart in her eyes, he moved. He took four steps, enough to cross the room, wrap her in his arms and bury his face in her hair.

"Oh, God, Nat. Oh, God." He was cold and wet, and shaking. At the same time the feel of his arms around her, of his heart pounding against her own, was the most wonderful feeling Natalie had ever had in her life. And she wrapped her own around him and hung on.

"You mean it?" he muttered against her hair. "You're not just saying it?"

"Humoring you, you mean?" She was smiling now, turning her head to kiss his jaw, to rub her lips over the unshaven stubble of his cheeks.

He pulled back to look down at her, his forehead furrowed.

She smiled and shook her head. "Not humoring," she assured him. "Telling the truth. I've loved you…forever, it seems. Before I knew what I was doing, three years ago—"

"That wasn't love," Christo protested.

"No, it wasn't. It was attraction and hormones. And good taste," Natalie added with a faint grin. "But it's love now."

"Thank God," Christo breathed. He hugged her hard again. "My grandmother was right."

"What do you mean?"

Christo reached into his back pocket to pull out his wallet, then withdrew from it a folded piece of paper which he handed to her. With trembling fingers, Natalie unfolded it. It was a short letter in shaky handwriting written in Portuguese. Natalie looked at it helplessly.

"I'll read it to you." And Christo began to translate. "'My Christo,' it says, 'I love you for trying to make my last days the happiest in my life. I love you for...for bringing Natalie to meet me even though you are not really engaged to her. You may be a lawyer, Christo, but you can't fool your grandma. You must know that by now.'"

"She knew?"

"She understood," Christo said wryly. "She knew how I felt about marriage. About my parents. She knew me," he admitted.

His mouth twisted briefly. Then he cleared his throat and read on.."'But whether you know it or not, your heart has chosen her. And hers has chosen you.'"

"She saw the way I looked at you," Natalie said, remembering.

Christo nodded, then went on with the letter. "'Natalie will...will love you if you let her.'" He flicked a quick glance in her direction. "'I will not push you, my grandson—'" He stopped when his voice grew ragged and he took a breath before continuing. "'But I hope you will learn to trust your heart—and yourself. That will make me happiest of all.'" His throat seemed to close on the last words, and he swallowed convulsively.

And Natalie was aware of tears running down her cheeks. "She knew," she whispered.

And this time, somehow, it wasn't mortifying. It was heartening to know that Lucia had trusted her. It made her feel loved and, like Christo, understood.

She turned to him joyfully. "So we can give her another wedding—without the hassle of the last one?"

He shook his head sadly. "She died last Saturday." His voice faltered for a brief moment. "In my arms."

His vacation. His "space" had been his grandmother's deathbed.

He was a man so intensely private that he hadn't even told Laura where he was going or why.

Natalie wished she had been with him. She wished she could have apologized to his grandmother for their deception. She wished she could have thanked this amazing woman for seeing into her heart and understanding her, for recognizing her love for Christo—and giving it her blessing.

"I'm sorry. I'm so sorry. But I'm so glad I got to meet her. And I'm glad—I'm glad she knew." She put her arms around him then, holding him, loving him, rejoicing that at last she had the right to.

They stood rocking together, hanging on, remembering and cherishing the memories, comforting each other.

And then Christo said, "You're shaking." He stepped back. "You're freezing. And wet." He sighed and shook his head. "My fault."

"I know a way to get warm," Natalie said. And she took his hand and drew him with her into her small bedroom.

Had she fantasized having Christo there? Oh, yes. And she'd reveled in the fantasies. But the reality was so much better.

They undressed each other quickly, laughing now at their fumbling fingers and stumbling feet. And then they tumbled into the bed together and wrapped the duvet around themselves, curling together, cold damp bodies in their own cocoon—and warming up fast.

"Told you," Natalie said, nuzzling his jaw, kissing him, letting her hands wander over his naked body, and squirming when his did the same to her.

"Smart woman." Christo grinned. He shifted and

pinned her with one of his legs, then ducked his head under the duvet and began kissing her breasts, working his way down.

And Natalie, burning up now, luxuriated in his ministrations, reached down beneath the duvet to run her hands over his hair, then gasped when he reached the center of her. "Christo!"

She tugged, but he didn't let her go this time. He parted her legs and kept right on. Natalie bit her lip and shuddered under his touch. Her back arched as the feelings built. Her fingers fisted in his hair as the wave of her climax rolled over her.

And as she lay there, still shuddering, Christo lifted his head from beneath the duvet, looking supremely satisfied. "I've been wanting to do that for three years."

Natalie felt herself blush all over. "You haven't!"

It was one thing to have fantasies about him, but to imagine herself the object of his made her hot all over.

He rolled onto his back and drew her on top of him. "That's not what you wanted, turning up in my bed?" He was grinning up at her.

She wriggled experimentally, making him clench his teeth at the friction of her body against his still-hungry one. But even as she did so, she said quite honestly, "I wanted to love you."

His grin faded and he looked solemn as he nodded. He reached up and touched her cheek. "Which is exactly what I was afraid of." He gave her a wry look. "So I sent you away. But the seed was planted. The memory was always there. I couldn't quite get you out of my head."

Natalie grinned. "I'm so glad."

"I am too. Now."

"Did you—" she hesitated "—you know…really imagine us…me…" Now she was blushing again.

"Every time I saw you after that. You'd be visiting your mother, taking out her trash or just sitting there with that cat on your lap, and I'd be remembering you in my bed."

"Nothing happened in your bed!"

"You had been there. That's all I needed. I have a good imagination," he added drily.

And then he was kissing her again, wrapping her in his arms and holding her, cherishing her as if he'd never let her go. Natalie's eyes pricked with tears. She kissed him in return, then shifted to accommodate him and felt a sense of completion when he surged up into her.

His back arched and he sucked in a sharp breath and squeezed his eyes shut.

"Did you imagine this?" she asked him, smiling down on him, shifting slightly, rising, falling.

His breath hissed through his teeth. "Didn't…dare." His voice was ragged and his breath caught once more as she moved. "Would have…done me in."

Natalie laughed softly as she felt his body tremble beneath her as he gritted his teeth and clung to his control. "We wouldn't want that, would we? Not too often, anyway." And she smiled as she raised up, then slowly came down again, bending to kiss his lips as Christo rose to meet her.

His hands gripped her hips and he lifted her again, then drew her back down. Again. And again. Natalie felt her own need start to build. And when his head fell back, his whole body went rigid as his climax shattered him, and her own rippled through her, a slow exquisite sensation of being one with the man she would always love.

* * *

"I love you," Christo told her.

He could say it now easily. He said it daily. First thing in the morning, last thing at night. Often in between. And he meant every word.

The two months he'd been married to Natalie had been the best of his life. He was hers, heart and soul—*body* went without saying—and he didn't mind telling her so.

Naked, she smiled over her shoulder at him as she slipped out of bed. "I'll be right back."

"You'd better be." He smiled, too, and lay back against the pillows waiting for her. It was Saturday. There was plenty of time for a long lie-in—for more enjoyment of Natalie in his bed.

Sometimes he wondered if he'd been insane to send her away that night three years ago. Reflecting on the joy that was making love to Natalie, he wondered how he'd turned her away.

But if he hadn't, he knew he wouldn't have what he had now.

He would have had a night with her, a single memory of her. But he wouldn't have a future with her. He wouldn't have a wife. He certainly wouldn't have the blessing of Natalie's love.

He was the luckiest man alive, he reckoned—and believed it even more fervently when his wife reappeared.

He held out a hand to her and, smiling a little tremulously, she took it and slipped back into bed beside him. She kissed his chest, then looked up to meet his gaze. The look on her face was unreadable, one he'd never seen before. And used to being able to read her now, he felt suddenly alarmed.

"What's wrong?" he demanded.

And then, even as he watched, her smile changed and her face was suffused with such happiness that he blinked. "Nothing's wrong. Everything's wonderful."

Then he smiled, too, relieved to hear it. He drew her on top of him and wrapped his arms around her. "It is, isn't it?" He kissed her, a long kiss that lingered until she broke it, pulled back, drew away.

"It will be better," she told him. Her words were solemn, sounding almost like a vow.

Christo arched a brow. "Oh, yes?" His hand smoothed down her back and over her bottom. "I can't imagine how."

She closed the distance between them, kissed his lips, then smiled into his eyes. "You won't need any imagination," she told him, "about seven months from now."

It took him a moment to understand the implication of her words. His hand stilled. His breath caught. He raised his head from the pillow and looked into her smiling eyes. He swallowed down equal parts panic and elation.

"You mean it? You're…" He couldn't quite get out the word.

She nodded, eyes twinkling. "I am." She gave a little wiggle that had his blood pressure spiking. "I thought I might be. But I wasn't sure, of course. So I bought a kit. Just did a test." Another wiggle. Another spike.

Their eyes met. Their gazes locked. Natalie didn't speak, just waited for his reaction.

"That's—" he searched for the right word, and settled for honesty "—scary as hell."

"Are you sorry?" She pulled back, all worried concern.

But Christo didn't really even have to think about it. He shook his head, smiling. "Not sorry at all. Just terrified."

She laughed. "You'll be a wonderful father."

"I've had such a great example with my own," he said wryly. But he could forgive Xanti his failings now. They were in the past. They didn't matter anymore. Nothing mattered now except the woman in his arms and the children they would raise together.

"You will certainly be better than Xanti," Natalie agreed. "Though," she added generously, "he might do better this time."

The news that his father, at the age of fifty-four, was about to embark on fatherhood again had boggled Christo's mind when he'd first heard it. He'd felt instantly sorry for the child. But now he thought Natalie might be right.

After all, if he could grow and change and learn from Natalie loving him, perhaps his father was capable of learning new tricks as well.

"We can hope," he said. He tugged her on top of him and held her there so that their foreheads touched, their noses brushed, their lips met.

"I love you," Natalie told him.

"I love you, too," he said, and once more drank in the sweetness of her lips. Then, when she assured him that making love was still possible even if they were going to be parents in seven months, he did just that.

Afterward, when he held her in his arms, he kissed her again. "I never believed in any of this. Now I can't believe in life without it—without you. I don't ever want one without you."

Natalie returned his kiss wholeheartedly. "The feeling, my love, is mutual."

MILLS & BOON

SEPTEMBER 2009 HARDBACK TITLES

ROMANCE

A Bride for His Majesty's Pleasure	Penny Jordan
The Master Player	Emma Darcy
The Infamous Italian's Secret Baby	Carole Mortimer
The Millionaire's Christmas Wife	Helen Brooks
Duty, Desire and the Desert King	Jane Porter
Royal Love-Child, Forbidden Marriage	Kate Hewitt
One-Night Mistress...Convenient Wife	Anne McAllister
Prince of Montéz, Pregnant Mistress	Sabrina Philips
The Count of Castelfino	Christina Hollis
Beauty and the Billionaire	Barbara Dunlop
Crowned: The Palace Nanny	Marion Lennox
Christmas Angel for the Billionaire	Liz Fielding
Under the Boss's Mistletoe	Jessica Hart
Jingle-Bell Baby	Linda Goodnight
The Magic of a Family Christmas	Susan Meier
Mistletoe & Marriage	Patricia Thayer & Donna Alward
Her Baby Out of the Blue	Alison Roberts
A Doctor, A Nurse: A Christmas Baby	Amy Andrews

HISTORICAL

Devilish Lord, Mysterious Miss	Annie Burrows
To Kiss a Count	Amanda McCabe
The Earl and the Governess	Sarah Elliott

MEDICAL™

Country Midwife, Christmas Bride	Abigail Gordon
Greek Doctor: One Magical Christmas	Meredith Webber
Spanish Doctor, Pregnant Midwife	Anne Fraser
Expecting a Christmas Miracle	Laura Iding

0809 Gen Std LP

MILLS & BOON

SEPTEMBER 2009 LARGE PRINT TITLES

ROMANCE

The Sicilian Boss's Mistress	Penny Jordan
Pregnant with the Billionaire's Baby	Carole Mortimer
The Venadicci Marriage Vengeance	Melanie Milburne
The Ruthless Billionaire's Virgin	Susan Stephens
Italian Tycoon, Secret Son	Lucy Gordon
Adopted: Family in a Million	Barbara McMahon
The Billionaire's Baby	Nicola Marsh
Blind-Date Baby	Fiona Harper

HISTORICAL

Lord Braybrook's Penniless Bride	Elizabeth Rolls
A Country Miss in Hanover Square	Anne Herries
Chosen for the Marriage Bed	Anne O'Brien

MEDICAL™

The Children's Doctor's Special Proposal	Kate Hardy
English Doctor, Italian Bride	Carol Marinelli
The Doctor's Baby Bombshell	Jennifer Taylor
Emergency: Single Dad, Mother Needed	Laura Iding
The Doctor Claims His Bride	Fiona Lowe
Assignment: Baby	Lynne Marshall

0909 Gen Std HB

MILLS & BOON

OCTOBER 2009 HARDBACK TITLES

ROMANCE

The Billionaire's Bride of Innocence	Miranda Lee
Dante: Claiming His Secret Love-Child	Sandra Marton
The Sheikh's Impatient Virgin	Kim Lawrence
His Forbidden Passion	Anne Mather
The Mistress of His Manor	Catherine George
Ruthless Greek Boss, Secretary Mistress	Abby Green
Cavelli's Lost Heir	Lynn Raye Harris
The Blackmail Baby	Natalie Rivers
Da Silva's Mistress	Tina Duncan
The Twelve-Month Marriage Deal	Margaret Mayo
And the Bride Wore Red	Lucy Gordon
Her Desert Dream	Liz Fielding
Their Christmas Family Miracle	Caroline Anderson
Snowbound Bride-to-Be	Cara Colter
Her Mediterranean Makeover	Claire Baxter
Confidential: Expecting!	Jackie Braun
Snowbound: Miracle Marriage	Sarah Morgan
Christmas Eve: Doorstep Delivery	Sarah Morgan

HISTORICAL

Compromised Miss	Anne O'Brien
The Wayward Governess	Joanna Fulford
Runaway Lady, Conquering Lord	Carol Townend

MEDICAL™

Hot-Shot Doc, Christmas Bride	Joanna Neil
Christmas at Rivercut Manor	Gill Sanderson
Falling for the Playboy Millionaire	Kate Hardy
The Surgeon's New-Year Wedding Wish	Laura Iding

MILLS & BOON®

OCTOBER 2009 LARGE PRINT TITLES

ROMANCE

The Billionaire's Bride of Convenience	Miranda Lee
Valentino's Love-Child	Lucy Monroe
Ruthless Awakening	Sara Craven
The Italian Count's Defiant Bride	Catherine George
Outback Heiress, Surprise Proposal	Margaret Way
Honeymoon with the Boss	Jessica Hart
His Princess in the Making	Melissa James
Dream Date with the Millionaire	Melissa McClone

HISTORICAL

His Reluctant Mistress	Joanna Maitland
The Earl's Forbidden Ward	Bronwyn Scott
The Rake's Inherited Courtesan	Ann Lethbridge

MEDICAL™

A Family For His Tiny Twins	Josie Metcalfe
One Night With Her Boss	Alison Roberts
Top-Notch Doc, Outback Bride	Melanie Milburne
A Baby for the Village Doctor	Abigail Gordon
The Midwife and the Single Dad	Gill Sanderson
The Playboy Firefighter's Proposal	Emily Forbes

millsandboon.co.uk Community

Join Us!

The Community is the perfect place to meet and chat to kindred spirits who love books and reading as much as you do, but it's also the place to:

- **Get the inside scoop from authors about their latest books**
- **Learn how to write a romance book with advice from our editors**
- **Help us to continue publishing the best in women's fiction**
- **Share your thoughts on the books we publish**
- **Befriend other users**

Forums: Interact with each other as well as authors, editors and a whole host of other users worldwide.

Blogs: Every registered community member has their own blog to tell the world what they're up to and what's on their mind.

Book Challenge: We're aiming to read 5,000 books and have joined forces with The Reading Agency in our inaugural Book Challenge.

Profile Page: Showcase yourself and keep a record of your recent community activity.

Social Networking: We've added buttons at the end of every post to share via digg, Facebook, Google, Yahoo, technorati and de.licio.us.

www.millsandboon.co.uk